THE LONG A

"Buck, there's somebody in the back," Curlew cried. "There may be a whole gang of them!"

"Go see who it is," Hayes said.

But before Curlew could make a move, Ki arched his back, his right leg flew up and the gun in Hayes's hand flew toward the ceiling.

"God *dammit*!" the marshal muttered as Curlew drew back from Ki in alarm.

Ki got up on his hands and knees. Supporting himself on both palms, he extended his left leg, pivoted on his right knee while using his hands to maintain his balance, and swung his left leg in a sharp arc, knocking Hayes's legs out from under him.

The marshal went down hard, cursing all the way until he hit the floor. The wind was knocked out of him, which effectively silenced him.

Ki sprang up and made a run for it. But he never got into the back room. . . .

→ **WESLEY ELLIS** ←

LONE STAR

AND THE
DEATH MERCHANTS

J

JOVE BOOKS, NEW YORK

LONE STAR AND THE DEATH MERCHANTS

A Jove book/published by arrangement with
the author

PRINTING HISTORY
Jove edition / January 1989

ISBN: 0-515-09876-0

Jove books are published by The Berkley Publishing Group,
200 Madison Avenue, New York, New York 10016.
The name "JOVE" and the "J" logo
are trademarks belonging to Jove Publications, Inc.

PRINTED IN THE UNITED STATES OF AMERICA

10 9 8 7 6 5 4 3 2 1

Chapter 1

The eyes of all the men gathered in the huge common room of the Circle Star ranch were on Jessie Starbuck, daughter of Alex Starbuck the founder of the far-flung Starbuck business empire.

"Gentlemen," she was saying, her eyes alight with an emerald fire, "I want to compliment you all on your excellent efforts—and the superb results those efforts have produced for Starbuck Enterprises—during the last year."

Smiles blossomed on the faces of the men seated throughout the room. Heads nodded in acknowledgement of Jessie's compliment.

"I know the year ahead of us will be equally successful," she added.

"A far better year will it be," said the man seated closest to Jessie in his lilting Celtic voice that was, Jessie sometimes thought, a little like music.

"Always the boastful one, Liam, aren't you?" Jessie said with mock disapproval. In fact, Jessie found little to disapprove of in Liam McCoy. He was handsome, he was virile, and, though soft-spoken, a man of great strength,

1

both physical and emotional. She found him very attractive and was always pleased when he was in her company. His courtliness and intelligence were displayed like fine jewels that she could not help but admire.

"Ah, but it's not a bit boastful I am," Liam responded with raised eyebrows as he pretended surprise at Jessie's remark. "I'll lay a wager with the very Devil himself that my—our—Boston office will increase its net profit by a healthy seven to ten per cent in the next quarter. And beyond that—why, Jessie, even the sky's not the limit!"

"Such may well be the case—providing you can successfully conclude the deal with South Africa's Voorhees Diamond Mine," Jessie cautioned.

"I shall do so," Liam said simply, but both force and conviction were evident behind his words. "I have made contacts with certain parties in Antwerp, and it's as sure as sunrise am I that we will not only corner the market in top-of-the-line stones, but at a far-from-exorbitant whole-sale price."

Across the room—his eyes on Jessie as she watched Liam McCoy continue to talk enthusiastically of the coup he expected to accomplish in the international diamond market—the half-Japanese, half-American young man named Ki smiled faintly. It was apparent to him that Jessie was interested in Liam McCoy for more than mere business reasons. He wasn't surprised. Liam McCoy was a man who would turn the heads and flutter the hearts of most women.

Ki continued watching, his gaze shifting from McCoy to Jessie as they continued their animated conversation.

Jessie's long mane of hair, which was the color of ripe corn, glistened in the light from the fire that was blazing in the massive gray slate fireplace. At times, there were glints of copper in it, a legacy from her long-dead mother whose portrait—an attractive woman in a green gown who seem-

2

ingly watched and listened with interest to the conversation between Jessie and Liam McCoy—hung on the wall of the common room. Jessie's bright green eyes glowed, and there was a faint flush on her cheeks beneath their prominent bones. Even seated as she was now, it was easy for an observer to tell that her figure was what could be called statuesque: her breasts prominent, her hips full, but not at all ungainly, her legs long and lean. There was about her an aura of lush sensuality that was decidedly provocative, but in no way wanton. She was wearing a blue silk blouse, with narrow sleeves, that stretched taut across her breasts and a tailored black skirt that cinched at her waist, emphasizing her svelte figure.

Born to a Japanese woman and sired by the American master of a sailing vessel, who was one of Alex Starbuck's business associates, Ki tended to have a slightly different standard of beauty than most full-blooded Americans. But he would be the first to admit that Jessie Starbuck was a beautiful—indeed, ravishing— example of womanhood. She was, he thought surveying the room full of Starbuck Enterprises executives, like a brilliant flower blooming in a garden of cactuses.

"Ki?"

Ripped from his reverie by the sound of his name being spoken by Jessie, he said, "I'm afraid my mind was wandering. What did you say?"

"I asked if you thought it would be a good idea to transfer the assets of the Philadelphia Holding Company to Sinclair Associates in Arizona. Dade thinks it would be, since Sinclair is prospering with its copper mining and Philadelphia Holding is showing red ink on its balance sheet for the second year running."

"I respect Mr. Payne's judgement," Ki said with the slightest of bows in Dade Payne's direction, "and remind all present that I am not a businessman. But I wonder if one has a sick calf what is the best thing to do for it. Kill it? Or cure it?"

Jessie sat back in her wing chair, her hands resting on its plush velvet arms, and studied Ki. Then, turning to Dade, she asked, "What can be done to cut the holding company's losses? Further, what can be done to improve its earnings?"

"We could do one of two things—or both, when you come right down to it," Dade Payne answered.

"Those two things are?" Jessie prompted.

"Cut expenses and increase profits."

"Can you be more specific, Dade?" Jessie's hands came together, and she placed the tips of her ten fingers under her chin as she watched Payne pondering his answer.

She listened without interrupting as the man outlined ways to pare the staff of the Philadelphia Holding Company, to lease some of the square footage that it owned after physically consolidating operations following the reduction in the work force, and to institute a tight policy of control on the corporations for which Philadelphia controls and holds stock.

"'Tis not my bailiwick," began Liam McCoy, addressing Jessie, "but I would not think it amiss in such a situation to call for a cut in the operating expenses of each of Philadelphia's client companies. Say, five per cent across the board. That reduction in expenses could then be linked with an incentive program of some sort—cash bonuses with stock options, let us say—for key executives throughout the network that well might result in harder work on the part of those people who, in turn, could increase gross profits."

"And that gross profit," Jessie mused thoughtfully, "could wind up as a higher net as a result of the reduced expenditures throughout the system." Jessie paused and then asked Payne what he thought.

4

"I'm amenable. It would be a shame to liquidate the holding company actually. It has its finger on the pulse of some very important resources all up and down the Eastern seaboard."

"Do what must be done, Dade," Jessie said, with a quick glance at Ki. A look that meant she was pleased he had found a way that was not the least bit heavy-handed to take a positive approach toward solving the current, and hopefully temporary, financial problems of one of Starbuck Enterprises key elements.

The martial arts expert's face remained impassive, but he understood the meaning of Jessie's glance. There was little about Jessie he did not understand after all their years together, and that understanding was not always based on the words that passed between them.

Ki was a tall man, slightly over six feet, and when he moved it was with an almost feline grace. His well-muscled body hadn't an ounce of excess fat upon it, and his skin was smooth, despite signs of it having known wind and weather.

Despite the Oriental blood that blended with the Caucasian blood flowing in his veins, he could be mistaken at first glance for a full-blooded Caucasian. It was only on closer inspection, after a second or even third look, that one would recognize his foreign heritage in the shape of his light brown eyes. Those eyes were constantly watchful, often wary. His was the attitude of a warrior. In his case, the attitude of a trained and skilled Samurai warrior. A warrior who was skilled in the martial arts weapons and techniques not only of Japan but also of China and Okinawa. His straight, blue-black hair was worn shoulder length.

The brown sack coat he wore covered an immaculate white linen shirt, which was pleated in the front. Around his neck he wore a neatly knotted white cravat. His fawn-colored trousers were of wool, and the black ankle-high, flat-heeled boots he wore were so highly polished that they gleamed in the light of the fire.

He listened as Jessie and the others continued talking, silently practicing the art of *kime,* the focusing of all mental and physical energies—in this case mental energies—on the situation at hand. He did not want Jessie to catch him daydreaming again.

The talk was wide-ranging—from the harsh economics of shipping raw rubber from the Starbuck plantations in South America to west coast cities via the Cape of Good Hope, to labor problems in Starbuck forestry camps in Oregon, to the unsettling and steady rise in import duties, to the plans to expand the Starbuck cotton acreage in Georgia.

Though this was a business meeting, one of those held annually at the Circle Star, Ki noted that Jessie conducted it as if it were a social gathering of old friends. There was little or no tension. Instead, there was a kind of camaraderie that approached, at times, gaiety.

But business was being done. Decisions were made. Future courses were charted.

It was more than an hour later that a white-coated servant entered the room and, having caught his mistresses' eye, announced that dinner was served.

Ki was pleased as well as a bit amused to see that Jessie had managed to time the matter correctly. Business was finished for this day. Now the social side of the meeting could begin.

Jessie joined Liam McCoy and took his offered arm. As they started for the dining room, along with the others who were conversing in low tones behind them, Ki stepped up to Jessie and said, "If you will excuse me, I have some work to do."

"You'll not be joining us at dinner then?" Jessie asked, clearly surprised.

Ki shook his head.

"The rustlers?"

Ki nodded in response to her question, bowed and turned away.

Jessie watched him go and, when he had left the room, continued making her way toward the dining room. She was followed by the Starbuck executives who, in deference to her, had waited silently for her to make her move.

The dining table was bedecked with glowing candelabras and vases full of the wild flowers then in season. As the men fanned out around Jessie and Liam and began searching for their names on the engraved white cards that rested near the china and crystal place settings, Liam whispered, "Tell an old friend what it is that's wrong and worrying you."

Jessie started. "Wrong?"

Liam wagged a playful finger at Jessie as he escorted her to her place of honor at the head of the long table. "I felt your arm stiffen when Ki spoke to you just now."

Jessie relaxed. Smiled. "I should know better than to try to hide anything from you, Liam McCoy. You have a way of sensing my moods, of knowing almost exactly what I am thinking at any given moment. How ever do you manage to do it? You're as uncanny sometimes as Ki can be when he practices *mushin*."

"*Mushin?*"

"It's a kind of mental self-discipline, as I understand it, that helps a martial arts warrior like Ki to focus on the matter at hand—a battle perhaps—to the exclusion of all else. Ki calls it a state of "no-mindedness" that, he says, allows him to sense things not normally known or understood."

"Ah, I have no such skill as that, for which I am no doubt much the poorer than Ki. But what I do have is my

7

Celtic heritage which allows me to tune in, so to speak, to people's innermost thoughts and feelings."

"You make me uneasy, Liam. A woman does not want her innermost feelings and thoughts known to one and all."

As Liam drew back Jessie's chair and seated her at the table, he leaned over to whisper in her ear, "Not many men have that ability, my dear, so fret not. Then too, you know you have nothing to fear from me, even though my mother was a notorious Irish witch and my father a necromancer skilled in all the mystic Irish arts."

Jessie laughed lightly and, as Liam took his place on her right, said, "Now I know why it is that you were able to cast a spell over me almost from the first moment we met at the Boston office nine months ago, right after you had been hired."

"Isn't that a coincidence to shake the world in its very shoes, now?"

"What do you mean?"

"I mean *I* have been under the spell *you* cast upon *me* that day—the very instant—of our first meeting."

Jessie dropped her eyes momentarily and then once again met Liam's direct and somewhat suggestive gaze.

"Yes," he said, before she could speak again, "doesn't it seem indeed, my dear, that we have bewitched each other?"

Instead of speaking, Jessie gently rested her hand on Liam's hand.

He took her hand, raised it to his lips, and kissed it.

His lips lingered for a moment before he released Jessie's hand. Then, in a more business-like tone, "To get back to the matter we were discussing a moment ago. What is it that troubles you, Jessie, and what can I do to help?"

"We've been plagued lately with rustling here on the ranch," Jessie answered as a waiter placed an oyster cocktail seasoned with salt and cayenne pepper and swimming

8

in sherry wine in front of her. "It's nothing serious. Or at least it hasn't been up to now, but it is worrisome, of course. Some of the ranch hands have been searching for the rustlers, but they have had no luck so far in apprehending them. Ki told me earlier today that he intended to try his luck at running them down tonight, since they always work under the cover of darkness."

"You've been losing a lot of stock, have you then?"

"No, that's not the aspect of the matter that is troubling me," Jessie replied as she began to eat her oyster cocktail. "I'm worried about Ki. I don't want anything to happen to him. He is, after all, one man, and we don't know how many rustlers are involved in this operation. Each time the ranch hands went out after the thieves, they always went together—in groups of no less than five men."

"You're very fond of Ki, aren't you?"

"Oh, yes. We've been friends for years now. I have a great deal of affection for him. I like to think he feels the same way about me. I don't know what I'd do without him."

Liam speared an oyster from the cocktail he had been served and swallowed it before sighing and saying, "Ki is a lucky man."

Jessie gave him a sidelong glance of silent inquiry.

"I mean to say Ki is lucky to have such a beautiful woman for a friend. He's lucky to have you so close to him so much of the time. I hope you will take no offense at my country-boy manners, Jessie, and let me be bold and brash enough to say that I would give my eyeteeth to be standing in Ki's place."

"If you were tonight, Liam, you might also be standing in the path of a rustler's bullet."

As the waiter removed their cocktail bowls Liam said, "You know that's not what I meant, Jessie." He paused a moment before saying, "Ki sees you almost every day. I

9

see you twice, perhaps three times a year. Is there then to be no fairness in this cruel world of ours?" He lamented this with a deliberately theatrical roll of his eyes as he clasped a melodramatic hand to his forehead. "Ki basks in the sunlight of your presence all year long and I spend most of the year in utter darkness—the very direct and unhappy result of your absence from my life."

Bowls of cream of celery soup were placed in front of Jessie and Liam by a waiter.

"You're a terrible flatterer, Liam," Jessie said, before spooning some soup into her mouth.

"Do you mean terrible in the sense of 'ineffective' or terrible in the sense of 'offensive'?"

"I think you know very well what I mean."

"I thought women liked to be flattered."

"Oh, I suppose most women do. I'm not at all sure that I do though."

"What is it you do like, Jessie?"

She could feel the heat of desire rising within her for this decidedly attractive man with his black Irish good looks and old world charm, which had its roots in the rolling green hills of Ireland where he and his family had lived before the Great Potato Famine sent them literally running for their lives to the shores of America, and ultimately to Boston. But, she couldn't resist the opportunity to bait him playfully, "I like all sorts of things—a successfully consummated business deal, the crisp clear color of the light in October, good food, good friends—"

"May I count myself among the latter?" Liam asked, his voice suddenly husky, his soup forgotten. "Or do I misstep myself by wanting to consider myself your good friend as well as your employee and business associate?"

"Not at all, Liam. You know people who work for Starbuck Enterprises are considered more members of the family than they are employees." Jessie was sure she knew

10

what Liam was getting at but found herself oddly unwilling to admit openly to him that she did. She found herself equally unwilling to acknowledge the seductive dance that they had so naturally entered into. She wanted to see how he would proceed here in this room full of other men. All of whom, she knew, were intently watching her and Liam while elaborately pretending not to be doing so.

"Jessie, I don't know how to say what I want to say to you."

"What?" Jessie asked, pretending dismay. "The silver-tongued Liam McCoy is at a loss for words? Your Celtic ancestors would be ashamed of you for apparently failing to kiss the Blarney Stone before you left the old sod."

"You know I had planned to leave the ranch after dinner along with the rest of the men," Liam said, oblivious to the arrival of a huge roasted suckling pig on a silver platter that was placed in the center of the table to the delighted *ooohhs* and *aahhs* of the diners, Jessie among them. "I don't want to leave tonight, Jessie. I want to stay—with you," he added, his voice huskier than ever.

The man on Jessie's left, the head of Starbuck Enterprises Ottawa, Canada office, said something to his hostess. Jessie, turning away from Liam, answered him and then laughed in delight at something he said as he pointed to the pig, which had whole cranberries for eyes and was wearing a necklace made from fresh parsley.

Liam looked glumly down. Several minutes later, a waiter placed a plate containing several thick slices of pork before him and then filled his and Jessie's crystal goblets with sauterne. He shook his head when another waiter offered him a helping of julienne carrots from a steaming silver bowl. He took a warm roll from a basket and bit into it. Meanwhile, Jessie continued talking to the man on her left.

When his agony had reached a point that he found

nearly unbearable, it was abruptly wiped out by Jessie who turned in his direction and said, *sotto voce*, "Of course you will stay here with me tonight, Liam. And for as many nights after that as you think you can without risking damage to the affairs of the Boston office."

Liam sat frozen with delight and desire as he stared at Jessie and tried to make himself believe in the miracle of his sudden good fortune.

Without looking at him, she said only loud enough so that he would hear her, "I made the bad mistake of letting you get away from me the last time we were together in Boston. I don't intend to make the same mistake again tonight."

Liam McCoy suddenly knew what it meant to possess an embarrassment of riches as he stared at the stunning woman by his side who would, he now knew for sure, be in his bed before many more hours had passed, as she had been in his heart for so very long.

After a dessert of spicy baked apples accompanied by a sharp cheese and strong coffee, Jessie and the men who had dined with her retired, at her suggestion, to the common room where they were served an aged Spanish brandy in gleaming glass snifters.

"A toast, gentlemen, if I may," declared a thickly mustached man with the body of a whale as he rose and raised his glass. As Jessie held her glass in both hands and gently swirled the brandy it contained, the man, who was the chief executive officer of Starbuck Enterprises' import-export operation, continued, "To our lovely hostess and to another successful year for Starbuck Enterprises."

There were enthusiastic cries of *"Hear, hear!"* from several of the men; Liam McCoy was very much among them as he gazed with rapture upon Jessie who, as custom dictated, did not drink, since the toast had been, in part, in her honor.

Then, Jessie rose and raised her glass. As she turned first to one side of the room and then the other, she toasted her business associates. "I offer honor and my heartfelt gratitude to each and every one of you for all you have done for the success of our joint ventures. To you, gentlemen."

Then Jessie made her way among the men, pausing briefly with each small group to talk, to offer suggestions about their individual operations, and to listen to the important information they passed on to her.

Standing next to the fireplace, Liam McCoy watched Jessie progress through the room. She was a beacon burning bright among the somber and generally drab men. He wanted to rush across the room, to seize her, to rip the clothes from her body, and to . . .

He forced himself to look away from her and to join a group of three men who were hotly arguing the merits and demerits, as they understood them, of the nation's controversial gold standard.

Then, after what seemed like an eternity to Liam McCoy, it was over. The brandy snifters were empty. The last cigar had been smoked. Farewells were being said at the massive front door of the ranch.

Liam bade goodbye to his colleagues. When asked if he were coming with them to the train depot, he murmured something about his departure not being scheduled until the following morning. He could tell by the looks on the faces of some of the men and the glints in some of their eyes that his reply raised more questions than it answered.

Finally, the last carriage departed, and Jessie closed the front door. She stood with her back leaning against the door, her hands clasped in front of her, and her eyes on Liam as servants moved quietly about straightening the room and, in the dining room, removing the remains of the meal.

Jessie came away from the door. She picked up a

lighted candle in an ornate pewter holder. Then, she took Liam by the hand and led him out of the room and up the stairs to the second floor.

He held her hand tightly—wanting to kiss it—wanting to kiss her. He did neither but simply followed her into a large bedroom. Someone had turned back the bed's coverlet and a corner of a satin sheet. A dressing gown of pale blue chiffon lay on the bed. Beside the bed on the floor, were a pair of dainty slippers covered in blue moire silk.

When Jessie let go of his hand, Liam closed the bedroom door. He crossed the room and took her in his arms.

Their lips met.

Jessie's hands roamed up and down his back and down over his firm buttocks as their kiss continued. She raised her hands to his face, placed her palms against his cheeks and parted her lips, allowing his tongue to slip past her teeth. As it did, she moaned softly.

Then she withdrew from Liam and stepped backward. "I wanted you so badly when we met last in Boston," she said. "But you seemed so distant then, almost cold. Why did you shut me out, Liam?"

"I didn't," he protested as he began to unbutton her blouse. "I mean I—if I seemed cold to you, my darling, it was because of who you are and who I am. You the woman who heads the majestic Starbuck empire of business interests, and me an Irish lad only recently hired as an assistant to the assistant manager of Starbuck's Boston office. Ah, it was not my place to make calf eyes at such a lady as yourself." His last sentence had been couched in a parody of an Irish brogue.

Jessie slipped out of her skirt. "Then why tonight, Liam? What emboldened you tonight?"

"My place card."

"Your place card? I'm afraid I don't understand."

Liam, his eyes feasting on Jessie's magnificently lithe

14

body as she removed her embroidered white chemise and petticoat, answered, "I was sure you were the one who had seen to the seating arrangements as well as the dinner itself, no doubt. If I were right, then you chose to have me sit beside you. 'For what reason?' I asked myself."

"And what did *yourself* answer?" Jessie said in a skillful imitation of Liam's accented speech.

"That God—or perhaps the dark Lord Lucifer—willing, you might have some—some feeling for me—some slight attraction to me."

Jessie, now naked, lay down on the edge of the bed. "You were right. I did choose the seating arrangements. I did choose you as one of my dinner partners. Carl Sorenson, the octogenarian on my left, was just camouflage."

Liam quickly stripped off his clothes, throwing them onto the seat of an upholstered chair, and kicked off his shoes. He pulled off his socks, dropped them, and joined Jessie on the bed. The instant he did so, her arms were around him and his hand was fondling her breasts. He ran his hand down her rib cage past her navel, it came to rest against her hot and already moist mound. As he cupped it in one eager hand, he grew hard. He rolled over on top of Jessie, and as he did so she threw her head back and slid her right hand between their bodies.

He groaned with pleasure as he felt her fingers close on his rigid shaft. He arched his back and raised his pelvis slightly in order to give her room to maneuver.

She surprised him by sliding out from under him and by forcing him down upon the bed where he stared up at her with lustful eyes. She straddled him and then slid down along his body until she was kneeling between his legs.

He groaned again and closed his eyes as she lowered her head and took him into her mouth. He lay there, luxuriating in the sensations she was causing to course through his entire body as her head rose and fell, rose and fell upon

15

him in a rhythm that almost brought him to a climax.

Suddenly, as if she knew how close to coming he was, Jessie released him and skillfully maneuvered her body until she had mounted him. Settling down on him, taking his entire length into her, she swiveled her hips, first this way, then that.

He opened his eyes and saw the faint smile on her face.

"You're—you're—" he searched for the word, the right word that would define what she was to him at that moment. It never came to him, lost as he was in a sea of sensations that were raging within him as Jessie bucked wildly above his quivering body.

He raised his head and took her left breast in his mouth. His tongue flicked over its nipple. His lips suckled. He moved to her right breast and repeated the process. He felt himself about to explode . . .

But Jessie again slowed her movements while keeping him locked within her, and his climax did not occur. Then moving slowly, but with fierce intensity, Jessie began again to bring him to the point where he would find release. She kept at it until he was nearly maddened by the sensations she was stirring to a fever pitch within him. Each time— and there were four in all—she brought him to the brink and then back from it.

The fifth time she brought him to a climax that caused his body to shudder so violently it shook the bed, despite their combined weight that was pressing down upon it. A moment after he had flooded her, she too climaxed. As she did so, she gave a series of little cries interspersed with moans of pure pleasure. Her head was thrown back; her long hair hung down behind her, her lips were parted, and her skin glistened with a sheen of sweat in the candlelight.

Liam was able only to moan with pleasure as his body stilled somewhat and Jessie lay down beside him on the bed. Then he turned to her and said, "It would seem, my girl—" he paused to catch his breath, "—that your witchery is even more powerful than I would have dreamed possible. Jessie, love, you're a woman a man would consider the world well lost for."

She touched his lips with the tip of her right index finger. "I'm no witch, Liam. It's just that you are a very desirable man and I wanted to give you as much pleasure as I could."

"And it's that you did, love, that you most certainly did indeed. Were I a warlock, I could not have conjured up a more wonderful woman to warm the heart of a man like me." He kissed the tip of her finger.

"Was it only your heart I warmed, Liam?"

He parried her teasing remark with, "Forget my heart for the moment. What you warmed almost melted from the heat of your fire."

"Now that would be a shame! I shall have to be more careful next time."

"Don't you dare be careful!" Liam cried laughingly as he embraced her.

A few minutes later, they coupled again, and Jessie was not at all careful, making Liam a happy man as he gladly burned in the fire that her desire for him had once again kindled.

Chapter 2

Ki rode in a straight line just below the top of a ridge, close enough to see over its crest to the land below without the risk of being silhouetted against the sky by the bright moonlight.

The horse under him was a big-barreled buckskin gelding, his favorite among the Starbuck mounts because it had good wind and wasn't a biter.

He scanned the land on both sides of the ridge as he rode, picking out landmarks, looking for a sign of anything that did not belong in the area whether man, wagon, or horse, and listening for any sound that was made by anything that was not a natural part of the night.

He had chosen a scuffed and battered saddle belonging to one of the ranch hands, instead of the new one given him as a present last Christmas by Jessie, because on this job and on this night he didn't want the creaking of a new saddle to alert anyone to his presence on patrol of the ranch's grazing land. The one he was seated in now had been broken in long ago and no longer made any sounds.

He had changed his clothes before leaving the ranch. He

now wore a faded pair of blue jeans that were threatening to give way at the knees any minute from rough wear and tear, and as he had jokingly told Jessie, "let me out and the wind in." His bib shirt was brown; his low-heeled army boots were black, and his brown leather vest had in its pockets eight potentially deadly *shuriken,* or throwing stars, each with five blades sharp enough to slice into wood.

In the near distance, a wolf howled a message to the moon. Farther away, another wolf howled a mournful response.

As Ki rode on over a stretch of level ground that gave way up ahead to frost-cracked granite, he moved his horse downhill to avoid traveling over the rocky ground ahead which would make for a noisy passage that might alert anyone hidden in the night to his presence. After skirting the stony ground, he turned the horse again, riding uphill until his head and shoulders cleared the ridge and he could see clearly the land that lay to his right. It was a rough patchwork of ocotillo and cenizo shrubs beneath and around which grew short grasses, made even shorter this season because of the little rain that had fallen in the area during the past two months.

It was nearly an hour later that Ki heard the sound he had been expecting. He drew rein and sat still in the saddle, listening to the steady *clup-clup* sounds made by a horse traveling over an expanse of hardpan. Ki could tell by the sound, by its depth and its rhythm, that what he was hearing was no amorous wild mustang roaming around in the Texas night. No, this horse bore a rider. He continued to sit motionless in his saddle, listening, watching. He stared due north, the evening star visible in his peripheral vision as was the flight of an owl that swooped sharply and then rose again into the air, a hapless desert rat squealing in its talons.

The horse and rider Ki had been expecting appeared. They were down at the foot of the rise, heading due south.

Ki put heels to his horse and crested the ridge, pausing for a moment so that the rider down below would see him and perhaps, even at this distance, recognize him. If the rider didn't, he might go for his gun first and introduce himself later. Ki's gaze never left the man, never wavered. When he saw the man's right hand leave the reins, he got ready to make a move but the man picked up the reins again, thus making a move on Ki's part unnecessary.

Ki rode down the slope and joined the man who was waiting for him at the bottom.

"Evenin', Ki" the man said in a voice that had been made harsh by too many cigarettes.

"Evening, Tom."

"You shouldn't ought to sneak up on a man like that, Ki. When I spotted you up there on the ridge, I was all set to go for my gun. Would've too if I'd not seen who you was in time. Don't that moon make the night bright though?"

"I didn't want to call out to you, Tom. No telling who else might hear me."

"It's been quiet," Tom told Ki. "No sign of men with long ropes," he added, using the colloquial term for cattle thieves. "How come you're out here tonight?"

"I thought I'd have a look around," Ki replied. "See if I could stir up some rustlers."

"Maybe you and me should stick together until we run into Long Lou who's also out here line riding tonight like me, only he's riding counterclockwise. I figure I'll meet up with him in about another hour, maybe a little less."

"I'm heading over that way," Ki said, pointing to the northeast. "The rustlers haven't hit that part of the range and I think it's possible that's where they might strike next."

20

"Well, you got to do whatever you think's best, I reckon. I won't ask you to ride with me again, but it sure as hell is a lonesome job, line riding. I sure don't know why I chose to be a cowboy and court cattle for a living. Here I am out here with only Long Lou to keep me company, and both of us living the unhappy lives of two buck nuns."

Ki smiled and said goodnight to Tom. As he started to ride off in a northeasterly direction, Tom called out to him, "Ki, I'd be much obliged to you iffn' you should run into a bunch of strays over that way thereabouts, you'd herd them south to where the main herd is bedded down. I've been trailing 'em but lost track of 'em back aways."

"I'll do that, Tom. You take care."

"Same for yourself, Ki. Those rustlers ain't gone violent on us yet, but that's no doubt on account of how they haven't met up with any of us Starbuckaroos yet."

As Ki moved his horse out, Tom called out, "How come you ain't packin' no iron, Ki?"

"I seldom do," Ki called back, aware that his words were not really an answer to Tom's question. He smiled to himself as he heard Tom mutter to himself, "Foolhardiness, pure and simple."

Ki rode on, walking his horse, his ears attuned to the sounds of the night, his eyes keenly scanning the countryside ahead of and around him. It was the sound of cattle lowing nervously that alerted him to possible trouble up ahead. He halted his horse momentarily until he was sure of the direction from which the sound was coming—toward him from the north. He dismounted when the sound grew louder and led his horse behind a ragged clump of ocotillo bushes, where he ground-hitched his buckskin by looping the reins around the horse's right front leg. He stood for a moment in the shadows of the bushes and then, crouching, made his way in a darting, zig-zag course to-

21

ward the approaching cattle, which were still not visible but coming closer all the time.

Why, he asked himself as he moved erratically but with a destination in mind, would cattle—a lot of them judging by the volume of sound they were making—be moving now when they should be bedded down. Ki glanced at the polestar gleaming in the sky above him and, judging by its position, estimated the hour to be somewhere between midnight and one o'clock in the morning—the Hour of the Rat.

When the cattle came into sight, Ki halted his advance and crouched down behind the ruin of a fallen shin oak tree. He remained motionless as he watched the cattle come into sight, the longhorn in the lead swinging its immense horns from side to side as it lumbered lowing through the darkness. He ignored the two men riding on the right and left flanks of the herd as his eyes roamed over the cattle's hides. He had difficulty making out their brands, but he finally succeeded in doing so as one of the longhorns lunged to one side and ran toward him, only to be cut off by the rider on the animal's flank.

The brand on the beast, Ki had seen, was a circle within a circle, not the Starbuck ranch's circle enclosing a star. But they were Starbuck cattle all right. Ki had no doubt of that. Ki had seen proof of that fact on the longhorn's hide and had smelled it drifting on the cool night air.

He rose as the herd neared his position and stepped boldly out from behind the deadfall that had given him cover.

"What the hell—!" from the man who had reclaimed the would-be stray when he saw Ki materialize, a silent apparition in the night.

Ki ignored the man as he stood facing the oncoming herd. Concentrating hard, he managed to catch the eye of the steer that was leading the others. As he did so, the

22

animal's gait faltered but continued moving forward, though more slowly. Ki stood his ground, his eyes locked on the steer's that now began to blink, betraying its confusion at the sight of this man standing in its path.

Stop. The word thundered through Ki's mind but his lips did not speak it. *Stop!*

The steer tried to turn but couldn't.

Ki held up a hand as the longhorn looked back at him. *Stop!*

The steer, as if hypnotized, stopped.

The cattle behind the animal moved forward a few paces before they too stopped.

Ki looked up at the rider nearest to him. The man wore a sidearm, an Army Colt .45. The man's hand rested on the butt of the gun. The man opposite him on the other side of the herd was armed with a Smith & Wesson Schofield revolver.

"Get the hell out of the way!" roared the man nearest to Ki.

"You men trail drive at night as a general rule, do you?" Ki asked in an even voice.

"What business is that of yours?" the man with the Army Colt shot back.

"It's my business because I'm from the Circle Star ranch and you've stolen some of our cattle."

"You're crazy, mister!" yelled the man on the far side of the herd. "These are our stock."

"I'd appreciate it if you would show me a bill of sale," Ki said quietly.

"Bill of sale, hell!" the man who had just spoken bellowed. "We bought these here steers a month ago up over the line in the Nations. We don't carry a bill of sale around with us for a month. You—"

"Easy, Rafe," said the man nearest to Ki. "I'll handle this."

"You ought to shoot him, Reardon. He called us thiefs. You heard him."

The man named Reardon held up a hand to silence Rafe. "Now, mister, I got just two things to say to you. One, you get out of our way and let us get on about our business. Two, you don't and I'll let light through you."

Ki, undeterred, walked slowly closer to Reardon. He pointed to one of the steers near him. "That your brand, the Double Circle?"

"It is."

"It's not. You're a liar, Reardon."

"Why, you—"

As Reardon drew his gun, Ki seized the man's lower leg with both hands, twisted to the left, pulled, then jerked, and Reardon came flying out of the saddle to land with an audible thud at Ki's feet. Almost before the man had hit the ground though, Ki was turning back, bending down, and reaching with his right hand. He disarmed Reardon, stepped back and straightened up, holding the gun on the man he had downed.

Reardon, slightly stunned from his fall, blinked wordlessly up at Ki. Then, regaining the power of speech, he said, "Drop him, Rafe! Kill him!"

Ki dropped to the ground, rolled over in a forward somersault, and came up in the midst of the cattle. He held Reardon's gun steady in both of his hands and aimed directly at Rafe, whose mouth hung open and whose eyes were wide with surprise.

"Drop it," Ki said calmly, his eyes locked on Rafe's.

Rafe's finger tightened on the trigger of his gun, but at the ominous sound of the click made by Ki drawing back the hammer of Reardon's .45, he dropped his weapon, which was immediately lost to sight beneath the hooves of the now milling longhorns.

Ki was about to turn so that he could keep his eyes on

both Rafe and Reardon when he felt something hard slam into the middle of his back.

"Gimme my gun."

The words were like stones thrown at Ki who realized, with chagrin, that he never should have turned his back on Reardon, even though the man had been stunned by his hard fall from his horse.

"I always pack a hideout gun," Reardon said. "It comes in handy when you run up against some slick son-of-a-bitch such as yourself."

In an attempt to distract the man, Ki raised his hands high above his head and dropped Reardon's revolver. Then he said, "You blotted the Circle Star brand on these steers. You used a solid circle brand to blot out the star inside the circle, so that you ended up with a Double Circle brand. But your brand blotting's easy to spot. The inside circle is still raw from the branding iron, and those burned hides still stink to high heaven. I smelled it even before I caught sight of you."

"You're right, but that's not going to do you one damn bit of good, mister," Reardon snarled.

On the far side of the herd, Rafe dismounted and yelled, "My gun! These beeves are stomping it into nothing but a piece of bad-bent iron!"

Ki swiftly shifted his weight to his right foot and spun his body counterclockwise. At the same time, he dropped his right elbow and diverted Reardon's right forearm away from him by a sweeping blow of his arm. He then grabbed Reardon's gun-hand wrist with his left hand, reached under the weapon, and grabbed the barrel with his right hand.

Holding his left hand close to his body for more power, he pushed the gun barrel up and forward, forcing Reardon to release his hold on the weapon. Ki swung the gun by the barrel, smashing it across the right side of Reardon's face. Reardon's body bent backward toward the ground. Turning his palm downwards, Ki then slammed the left side of Reardon's face with the gun. Reardon let out an anguished howl and fell backwards onto the ground.

Ki retrieved Reardon's gun and placed it in his waistband before stepping back to avoid any possible retaliatory moves on Reardon's part, although he was reasonably confident that Reardon was in no condition to attack him at the moment. As he did so, he saw Rafe watching him with an awestruck expression on his face. Then Rafe realized that Ki was watching him and that Reardon was in no condition to continue the battle. Rafe slammed a foot into a stirrup and was just about to swing into the saddle when Ki raced nimbly through the milling cattle and seized him from behind. Ki's left forearm went around Rafe's neck in a stranglehold. He used the knuckle of his right thumb to apply a steady and potentially fatal pressure to an area just below Rafe's left ear—just enough to induce unconsciousness, but not enough to stop the man's heart.

As Rafe went limp, he released his cross-collar chokehold, picked the man up bodily, and threw him facedown across his saddle. Then, turning, he saw that Reardon was struggling to his feet. He rounded the herd and confronted the rustler.

"You can travel the way your friend over there is traveling or you can ride in front of me. If you choose the latter, be warned. If you make one wrong move, you'll regret it—but not for long because that wrong move will have shortened your life considerably. Let me guarantee you. Which is it to be?"

"How'd you kill Rafe? With a knife? I didn't hear a shot."

"I didn't kill him but I could have—and not with a knife. I put him out of action with this." Ki held up his right thumb and crooked it to display its knuckle.

"How—"

26

"I slowed his heart rate. He'll recover in a few hours when his blood flow returns to normal. Now, let's go."

They went to where Ki had left his buckskin. Ki mounted his horse and, trailing Rafe's horse that bore its rider's body draped across the saddle, he moved out. A weaponless and thoroughly intimidated Reardon rode docilely in front of him.

Morning came to the Starbuck ranch, bringing with it birdsong and the scent of honeysuckle drifting on the light breeze.

Jessie stirred in her bed and then remembering the antics of the night, smiled faintly without opening her eyes. "Liam," she whispered. When there was no answer, she whispered his name a second time.

When she still received no answer, she opened her eyes and turned on her side. He lay there beside her, his black hair tousled, his bare chest rising and falling rhythmically.

She leaned over and kissed his cheek.

He stirred. Stretched. And then reached for her hungrily, pulling her down upon him, his lips searching for and finding hers. Their kiss lasted a full minute.

Then, as their lips parted, Jessie said, "Welcome to the world."

He turned his head toward the window and said, "It's morning."

"Time to be up and doing."

"I'd rather stay here and do it."

"I've no doubt at all that you would, but that's not what I meant and you know it."

Jessie climbed out of bed and went to the mahogany dresser on which rested a flowered porcelain basin and a pitcher of water.

By the time they had both finished their morning ablutions and were dressing, the sun was well on the way toward its meridian.

"I should have been up hours ago," Jessie said, feeling a slight twinge of guilt.

"I could have slept for another hour or two," Liam volunteered. "You just about wore me out last night, love."

"It's your own fault," Jessie countered. "You're a very handsome man, and you drove me wild with desire."

"I can't wait until tonight," Liam said with an exaggerated leer as he pulled his braces up over his shoulders.

They went down to breakfast, and Jessie inquired of the servant who poured the coffee whether or not Ki had returned. He had not, according to the servant.

Jessie found the news unsettling. So unsettling, in fact, that though ravenous after the long and lusty night of lovemaking with Liam, she ate very little.

Liam, on the other hand, devoured the fried steak and boiled potatoes that were set before him and made short work of a stack of pancakes. He finished his meal with two hot, lavishly buttered corn muffins and two cups of strong scalding coffee.

Only then, when his hunger was fully tamed, did he notice that Jessie had eaten very little. She was now merely toying with a poached egg that was growing as cold as the toast on which it rested.

"What is it, Jessie?" he asked her. "You're not having regrets, I hope, about last night?"

Distracted, she did not at first hear what he had said, but when he repeated his question, she shook her head.

"Then you must be worrying about Ki."

"Yes," she admitted, "I am."

"From what I've heard of his exploits and his skill in the martial arts, I doubt very much that you have anything to worry about. Ki could probably take on a whole troop of rustlers and come out the winner."

28

"I'm sure you're right," Jessie agreed. "But I thought he would have been back long before this."

"These muffins," Liam said—trying to tempt her into eating something—"are absolutely delicious. They equal those of Delmonico's in New York, I swear. Have one." He offered Jessie the napkin-covered wicker basket in which the muffins rested, but she declined to take one.

Instead, she rose and went to the window where she stood staring out over the rolling land that stretched away from the ranch house to the far horizon. There was no one within her line of vision.

Not at first. But then, topping a rise off to the right was a lone rider. Jessie, suddenly animated, said to Liam without turning around, "Here he comes now."

Liam joined her at the window and put his arm around her waist.

As he did so, she said in a voice thick with disappointment, "No, that's not Ki."

"Who is it?" Liam asked, his eyes on the rider who was rapidly approaching the ranch house.

"It's Ty Hickham, one of our ranch hands," Jessie answered.

She went to the front door and opened it as Hickham drew rein and dismounted.

"Good morning, Miss Starbuck," Hickham said as he touched the brim of his hat to her.

"Good morning, Ty. Is something wrong?"

"No, Miss, nothing's wrong. I just come from town. I was in there placing our weekly order at the Feed and Grain—oh, by the way, old Witherspoon there said to tell you they got in some top-grade bran that you might like to try since it don't cost but two cents the pound more than his regular bran."

Jessie suppressed her growing impatience as she waited

for Hickham to get to the reason for his coming to the house.

Finally, after filling her in on the fact that Miss Harriet Soames, who ran the post office out of the general store, was getting married and that Sid Malone, the blacksmith was laid up from a kick to the hip given him by the widow Lederer's mare he was shoeing, he dug into the pocket of his levis and pulled out a sealed envelope which he handed to Jessie.

"Miss Soames done give me that when I stopped to check iffn' there was any mail for us, Miss Starbuck. Cyrus from the telegraph office, he left it with her she said."

"Thank you, Ty."

Hickham again touched the brim of his hat to Jessie before getting back on his horse and heading for the bunkhouse.

Jessie closed the door and returned to the window in the common room. She opened the envelope Hickham had given her. It was addressed to her. As she read it, her body tensed.

Brent died this morning. Please come if you can.
Need you desperately.

Theresa Latrobe

Liam, seeing Jessie's face grow suddenly and alarmingly pale, went to her and took her in his arms. "Bad news?" he asked, holding her close to him.

"Yes." The word was spoken in a forlorn voice.

Liam waited for her to explain.

Finally, getting a grip on herself, she withdrew from his embrace and wiped her eyes. Then she said, "An old and very dear friend of mine is dead. This telegraph message is from his widow. Her name is Theresa Latrobe—Tess, we

30

all called her. She wants me to come to her and, of course, I must go at once."

"Shall I come with you, Jessie?"

Jessie hesitated, wanting to say yes, wanting—needing—Liam's strength now to help her withstand the overpowering sense of loss she was experiencing at the ugly news of Brent Latrobe's death. But she shook her head.

"I don't know how long I will have to stay with Tess, Liam. I don't know what help she might need from me or what I might have to do to provide that help. I think you had better return to Boston now, since I will have to leave for El Paso—the Latrobe ranch is in that vicinity—as soon as possible."

Liam, though obviously disappointed at Jessie's decision, said, "You're right, of course. I would be remiss if I did not put first things first by which I mean my responsibilities to Starbuck Enterprises."

"I must pack," Jessie said in a hollow voice. "I just can't believe Brent Latrobe is dead," she said sorrowfully as she touched Liam's hand and then moved away from him, heading for the stairs. "I always thought of Brent as indestructible, just as I did with my father."

It was just afternoon when Ki returned to the ranch. He led his buckskin into the barn where he stalled it and stripped his gear from it. Then he watered the animal and filled the stall's feed bin with a mix of grains. As the horse ate, he carefully wiped the sweaty animal down.

He was on his way to the house when he saw Jessie and Liam leave it and stand, with their hands locked together, beside a buggy parked in front of the door. He halted and watched them exchange words. He continued watching as Jessie pressed her cheek against Liam's chest and Liam held her, his head bowed, his lips kissing the top of her head.

Then they parted, and Liam picked up the leather suitcase at his feet and placed it on the buggy's seat. He climbed into the conveyance, picked up the reins, and slapped them on the rump of the horse, which was standing nearly motionless in its shafts. The horse trotted forward, and as it did so Liam leaned out of the buggy and waved farewell to Jessie.

She watched the buggy grow smaller and smaller in the distance. As she turned to reenter the house, she caught sight of Ki standing some distance away. She ran to him and breathlessly asked him if he was all right.

"I am," he answered.

She told him how worried she had been about him, and then he told her that he had captured the two rustlers who had been plaguing them.

"What did you do with them?"

"Took them into town and left them in the care of Marshal Bowen. I told the Marshal he was welcome to come look at the brands they had blotted on our stock any time that was convenient for him. He assured me he would do so at his earliest opportunity."

"Then I went back to where I'd left the stock the rustlers had been driving when I ran into them and drove them back to the main herd. I left word at the line shack east of Broken Back Ridge for the hands to blot out the altered brands and then to brand those beeves with the Circle Star again in a different spot."

"It sounds as if you had a very busy night. Did you have any—uh, difficulties with the men you captured?"

"We did have a misunderstanding."

"A misundertanding?"

"They thought because I carried no gun that I would be no match for them. I cleared up that misundertanding."

As the pair walked toward the house, Ki commented,

"Jessie, you look pale and a bit drawn. Aren't you feeling well?"

"I'm fine." She looked off into the distance and then said, "No, that's not true. I'm not fine. Ki, I received a telegraph message this morning from Tess Latrobe. Brent Latrobe is dead."

"Dead? What happened?"

"Tess didn't say. But she did ask me to come to the Latrobe ranch near El Paso. She said she needed my help desperately. I was in the middle of packing for the trip when I had to stop to bid goodbye to Liam McCoy. He's returning to Boston this afternoon."

"Then you're going to the Latrobe spread?"

"Yes. On the first train out in the morning. Will you come with me?"

"Yes," Ki answered without hesitation. "I would like to have the opportunity to pay my last respects to Mr. Latrobe. He was always very nice to me, the few times we met."

"Brent Latrobe was one of the finest men I ever knew. I first met him years ago when he was working with my father in the Starbuck export-import business. I was only eleven at the time. He was a courtly man, a charmer. I fell in love with him by the time I was twelve and fully intended at that time to marry him when I grew up. He was single then. Later, after he had married and I had matured, his wife and I used to joke about that childish fantasy of mine. Oh, Ki, I find it hard to imagine the world without Brent Latrobe in it."

Chapter 3

Jessie and Ki sat side by side in the first-class coach as the Texas and Pacific train thundered along its tracks through West Texas on its way to El Paso. Both of them wore linen dusters as a protection against the omnipresent soot and dust that plagued train passengers. The dust was a nuisance; the occasional sparks that flew through the open windows were a potential danger. The latter, on occasion, had been known to set unwary passengers' clothes afire.

As the news butcher, an elderly man wearing a striped apron, entered the car, Ki turned to Jessie, who looked as if she were sleeping as she sat back in her adjustable seat with her eyes closed and her arms folded across her chest. "Can I get you something?" he asked her.

Jessie stirred and opened her eyes. Seeing the news butcher, she said, "I'd like a bottle of milk."

Ki beckoned to the news butcher. When the man came up to him, he bought two squat bottles of milk that were packed in ice in a corner of the man's tray, which hung by a strap from his scrawny neck.

"Can I interest the gentleman in some spicy reading

matter?" the butcher asked Ki in a stage whisper not meant for Jessie's ears as he counted out Ki's change. "Lookee here, sir." He lifted a soiled napkin and displayed a magazine with a lurid cover depicting a half-naked woman fighting off the obviously eager advances of a man, whose eyes the artist had depicted as wild if not downright demented. The title of the magazine, printed in large red letters above the struggling figures of the man and woman, screamed: *Velvet Vice*.

Ki shook his head.

"How about this one, sir?" persisted the butcher, displaying the equally lurid cover of a back issue of *The National Police Gazette*.

Unable to make the sale, the butcher moved on down the aisle, calling out his various wares: "Tin cups, wash basins, towels, soap, newspapers, magazines, sandwiches, ice-cold beer, Japanese fans for the ladies . . ."

His voice faded and then died as he moved into the emigrants' coach directly behind the first class coach.

Jessie finished drinking her milk and again leaned back in her seat and closed her eyes.

The train rumbled and rattled on, its couplings occasionally screeching. Despite the noise, Jessie drifted into a light sleep where dream images soon invaded her mind. She was a little girl again in a world of privilege. She was astride her first horse with Alex Starbuck, her beloved father, seated behind her in the saddle as he taught her how to control the animal.

The horse vanished. Alex Starbuck did too only to promptly reappear in the midst of what seemed to be a million beautifully gowned women and immaculately tailored men in the common room of the ranch house. Everyone was dancing to the music of a four-piece orchestra; the music soared to the rafters and brought delight to the little girl. Jessie watched the happy panorama unfold before her from the top of the staircase where she crouched in her lace-trimmed white nightdress.

A man appeared.

The man had salt and pepper hair and a bushy mustache. The smiling man with eyes like blue beads, who gave off the scent of lemon verbena, was climbing the stairs toward Jessie, a finger pressed to his lips to warn her to be silent. Then he sat down on the steps beside her and whispered, "Your daddy would scold if he knew his best beloved was out of bed at this awful hour—and spying on his guests to boot."

"You won't tell?"

"My lips are sealed," said the man in a stern voice before clapping both large hands over his mouth.

"Some day I shall dance down there," Jessie whispered in the man's ear.

"Some day?" he said, raising his eyebrows. "Why not now?"

"Down there?" she asked uncertainly, pointing to the men and women who were dancing a frisky Virginia reel now.

"Up here. Just the two of us."

Then he was standing on the second floor landing. She was facing him as he took her hands, and they danced, not a reel but a waltz that the man hummed for them alone.

When it was over, before he went back down the steps to join the other guests, he warned Jessie to hop into bed "to get your beauty sleep."

She threw her arms around his neck as he knelt before her and declared, "After Papa and Mama, I love you the very best, Mr. Latrobe!"

Jessie awoke with a start. Disoriented for a moment, she then found herself caught in a net of sadness that was the legacy of her dream about herself and Brent Latrobe in that long ago and now dead time. She became aware that her cheeks were wet with tears. She also became aware of the fact that Ki was watching her solicitously and silently holding out to her his neatly folded white linen handkerchief.

She took it from him and dabbed almost angrily at her eyes, damning the dream—the memory—that had just undone her.

"Excuse me, Ki. I'll be back shortly."

Ki rose to let Jessie out of her seat and watched as she made her way to the enclosed space at the end of the coach that passengers politely and intentionally vaguely referred to as the "convenience room", which was enclosed by closely-buttoned curtains.

He absently wiped his forehead with the handkerchief that Jessie had returned to him before leaving. He became conscious of the heat being thrown off by the iron wooden stove at the end of the coach opposite the convenience room. At the same time, he heard the faint sound of a woman singing in one of the other coaches.

Leaving the overheated coach he had been traveling in, he made his way into the one ahead of him, which turned out to be the parlor coach.

He stopped dead in his tracks as he entered the sumptuously appointed coach. But it was not the inlaid wall paneling, not the etched glass adorning the panels, not the bronze cherubs on the walls that were holding gilded sconces, nor the expensive bright red Brussels carpet underfoot that claimed his attention.

It was instead the woman who was standing beside a parlor organ, one dainty hand resting upon it, as she sang a melancholy love song about broken vows while a male passenger accompanied her on the organ.

Ki stood transfixed, his eyes locked on what he considered to be one of the most beautiful women he had ever seen, who was, he estimated, seventeen, perhaps eighteen years old.

37

Her auburn hair, the texture of fine silk, was piled high on top of her head and held in place with a tortoise shell comb. Her skin was so pale it appeared almost translucent. It glowed. Her eyes were brown, and as she sang, her left hand pressed against her ample bosom.

She wore no wedding ring, Ki noted. He also noted that her figure was superb. Enticing. Her provocatively flared hips spoke volumes about her femininity, as did the lush curves of her breasts, which the chambray traveling dress she wore could not disguise.

As his gaze roved up her figure to her face, their eyes met.

She almost missed a note but managed to recover and sing bravely and beautifully on.

Then she dropped her eyes, breaking contact. She continued, however, to stare at Ki, not at his eyes now, but at the bulging evidence of his erotic arousal that was blatantly evident between his legs despite the fact that he tried to shift his weight to hide his rampant erection.

The woman hit a high note. Her eyes flicked up and caught Ki's, and to his immense surprise and amusement, she gave him a grin that would have done credit to the Cheshire cat in *Alice's Adventures in Wonderland*.

Applause broke the woman's spell that Ki had fallen under. She acknowledged it politely, and despite the pleas of the other passengers that she sing another song for them, she made a graceful exit, quickly losing herself in the crowd she had just so successfully entertained.

Ki swore under his breath. Where had she gone? Where the hell was she? He elbowed his way, none too politely, through the crowd searching for her. Having just found her, he was not willing to lose her so quickly. She was, he discovered minutes later, not in the parlor car.

He made his way to the dining coach. It was empty.

He finally found her in the second class coach. He made

38

his way up to her and bowed from the waist as if he were greeting his *sensei,* his instructor, back in Japan in the *ryu,* the school where he had studied the martial arts. He then said, "I hope you will not think me forward, Miss, but I wanted to tell you how very much I enjoyed your singing. I particularly liked your choice of songs. It was one I had never heard before."

She looked speculatively up at him for a moment before saying, in a voice that Ki thought was so much richer than the voices of most American women—hers had timbre and resonance, "It's no wonder you found the song unfamiliar, sir. I wrote it myself. The gentleman accompanying me on the organ has only recently learned it. I taught it to him."

"The gentleman—he's a friend of yours?"

"An acquaintance. We met on the train. At Omaha."

"Ah, there you are, Opal!"

Ki turned at the sound of the hearty male voice as the gentleman they had just been discussing approached. He felt a sense of resentment toward the man and silently chided himself for it.

"You shouldn't have run off on us as you just did, my dear Opal," said the man, brushing past Ki and seating himself opposite the woman. "Your departure left us bereft. It was as if someone had turned the lamps down and left us in darkness."

Opal, smiling, reached out and patted the man's hand. "Such a silver-tongued devil you are, Matthew Keane."

Keane returned Opal's smile. Ki thought his smile had an oiliness, a slickness about it. He wanted to lift the man bodily, remove him, and take his place across from the lovely Opal.

Keane asked Opal if she would like to continue their "play."

Play? Ki wondered what Keane meant. Several possibilities occurred to him, almost every one of them bawdy.

39

"Oh, let's do, Matthew!" Opal cried, clapping her hands together. "You must be a gentleman and let me have a fair chance at trying to recoup some of my losses." She proceeded to set up a small folding table between herself and Keane.

Ki watched Keane reach into his pocket and withdraw a deck of cards.

Keane skillfully—even dramatically—shuffled the cards so that they seemed to blur. "I'm sure you'll beat this old badger at his own game this time out, Opal," he said. "But it may be that my hand is quicker than your eye. If that should indeed prove to be the case, you will lose." He frowned. He clucked sympathetically. He shook his head. Pocketed the cards.

"What's the matter, Matthew?" a clearly puzzled Opal asked him.

"I don't want to take advantage of you, my dear. I am ashamed of myself now for having let you play earlier when you lost a rather tidy sum."

"But Matthew," Opal protested, "I *want* to play again. You are not the least bit responsible if I should lose."

Ki wasn't so sure about that. But he said nothing, biding his time, watching Keane carefully.

Keane stubbornly shook his head.

"You are insulting me, Matthew," Opal said sternly.

He looked up at her. "I beg your pardon?"

"You are insulting me by not letting me pit my skill against yours. You are treating me as if I were a mere schoolgirl. I assure you I am not. I am a woman grown—"

A man with but one eye, and that one half-blind, could see that, thought Ki.

"—and as such I demand that you give me the opportunity to beat you, Matthew."

Lamb to the slaughter, thought Ki.

With a sigh, Keane capitulated on Opal's earnest argu-

40

ments. The deck reappeared in his hand and from it he selected three cards—the ace of hearts, the ten of clubs, and the deuce of spades.

"You remember how the game goes, don't you, Opal?" he asked.

She nodded, her eyes on the ace of hearts as Keane set the remainder of the deck aside. "You shuffle the three cards," she replied, "and I must be alert to where you have placed the—what did you call the ace of hearts when we played before, Matthew?"

"The baby card."

"Yes, the baby card. I must keep a sharp lookout and be able to tell you, when you have finished shuffling the three cards which one is the baby card."

"Right you are, my dear. Shall we begin?"

As Keane gave Opal a winning smile, Ki said to the man, "Sir, you are without a doubt one of the slickest broad throwers I've ever come across."

"How much do you want to wager, this time Opal?" Keane asked. He ignored Ki and kept his eyes on the cards that were flipping swiftly through his fingers.

"Ten—no, twenty dollars," Opal answered, withdrawing two gold double eagles from her reticule and placing them on the small table between her and Keane.

Keane, with a grand flourish, spread the three cards, facedown on the table. He looked expectantly up at Opal.

She touched the tip of her right index finger to her chin and then pointed it at the card in the middle. "That one," she said confidently, "is the baby card."

"You're quite sure?" Keane asked, his eyes narrowing slightly.

"I am quite sure."

Keane turned up the middle card to reveal the ten of clubs.

As Opal gave a sigh of defeat, he pocketed the two

41

double eagles she had placed on the table between them.

She grimly took another twenty dollars from her purse and placed it on the table, indicating with a glance at the gambler that Keane was to shuffle the cards again.

He did.

This time, when he was finished, Opal placed a firm finger on the card to his left. He overturned it to reveal the deuce of spades.

Ki, seeing that Opal's expression bordered on despair, could restrain himself no longer now that he was almost sure of what was going on, based on his close scrutiny of Keane's swift hands. Time to take the bull by the horns.

He reached out and turned over the middle card. The ten of clubs.

"I say, sir, what do you think you're doing?" Keane blustered as he tried to stay Ki's hand, which was reaching for the only remaining card. He grasped Ki's wrist, but Ki shook off his hand and turned over the third card.

Another ten of clubs.

"I don't understand," Opal said in a small voice, looking up at Ki.

"Keane does," Ki said. "Ask him."

"Matthew?" Opal prompted.

"There must be some mistake," Keane protested, addressing Opal while trying his best to ignore Ki. "I can't imagine what could have happened."

"I can do better than imagine what happened," Ki said. "I believe I can tell you exactly what happened to the baby card. You substituted it for the ten of clubs from another deck, Keane."

"Sir, I suggest that you mind your own business. This is a matter between the lady and myself."

Ki, ignoring Keane's protest, spread the remainder of the deck out on the table. "Where is it?" he challenged Opal.

She looked from him to the cards on the table. "Why, there is no ace of hearts here."

"Then where do you suppose it is?" he asked her.

Keane started to rise, his hand sliding under his broadcloth coat.

Ki thrust him back down in his seat and seized his right wrist, pulling his hand away from the hideout gun he had in a shoulder holster under his left armpit. Then he shook Keane's left arm violently. The baby card, the ace of hearts, fell out of Keane's sleeve and onto the table.

"See here—" Keane began, struggling to free himself from Ki's strong grip but failing to do so.

"How much have you lost to this tin horn gambler?" Ki asked Opal.

"One hundred and eighty-five dollars," she said in a voice that was almost inaudible from embarrassment. "And forty dollars just now."

"Give the lady her money back," Ki ordered Keane.

When the man hesitated, Ki ripped the derringer from the gambler's shoulder holster and aimed it at him. He said nothing. There was no need to say anything. Keane was fumbling in his pocket. He came up with Opal's two eagles first and placed them on the table. Then he brought out his purse, opened it, and looked at Ki.

Ki let go of the man. But he continued to hold the derringer on him.

Keane counted out one hundred and eighty-five dollars and placed it on the table.

"Take it," Ki ordered Opal who obediently scooped up the money and placed it in her reticule.

"We're going for a walk, you and I," he told Keane coldly. He hauled the man to his feet. "Hold onto this," he said to Opal as he handed her Keane's gun.

"What—" Keane began, but got no further. Ki was

43

manhandling him down the length of the coach, holding him tightly by the scruff of the neck.

Ki marched Keane through two coaches until he finally found the conductor to whom he gave a brief but complete description of what had been happening between Opal and the gambler.

Ki concluded with, "I understand the Texas and Pacific railroad has outlawed gambling on its trains for more than a year now."

"Yes, that's so," the conductor agreed.

"Passengers found engaging in such pursuits on a Texas and Pacific train are to be put off the train without a refund of the price they paid for their ticket. Is that correct, conductor?"

"Yes. We'll be pulling into Indian Junction in"—the conductor pulled a Swiss watch from his vest pocket and snapped it open—"in twenty minutes. I'll see to it that this gentleman leaves the train there."

"That won't be necessary," Ki said and pushed Keane out the door of the coach. Ki stood between the coaches with his feet planted firmly for balance. As the train slowed to round a bend up ahead, he hurled Keane from the train.

Behind him he heard a shocked cry. He turned to find Opal standing just inside the coach, holding the door open as she stared at Ki in open-mouthed shock.

Then the conductor appeared, not sure whether he should be irate as a result of Ki's actions or deferential because of the icy look in Ki's eyes. He chose deferential. "Good riddance to bad rubbish, sir," he murmured before hurriedly withdrawing.

Ki heard him muttering something about "the very real danger of a lawsuit against the railroad."

Ki stared silently at Opal. Her mouth slowly closed. Her

44

eyes began to shine. The corners of her lips turned up. She began to giggle, then to roar with laughter.

"Good riddance to bad rubbish," she said between uproarious bursts of laughter, repeating the words she had just heard the conductor say.

Gaining control of herself a moment later, she said, "I want to thank you, sir, for saving me from that despicable man's machinations. He duped me quite thoroughly, as you plainly saw."

"But you have your money back now," Ki pointed out. "And you are much wiser for your admittedly unpleasant experience."

"My name is Opal Hayes."

"Mine is Ki. I'm pleased to make your acquaintance, Miss Hayes."

"Please—Opal."

"May I escort you back to your seat?" Ki asked, offering her his arm.

Before she could take it, Jessie appeared in the opposite doorway and came running down the aisle toward them.

"Ki, someone said something about a man being thrown from the train and something else about there being an oriental man involved. I thought—the gossip I heard was so garbled—that it might have been you who had been thrown from the train."

"I wasn't thrown, as you can see, Jessie. I was the thrower."

Jessie caught her breath. Her gaze shifted to Opal, then, questioningly, back to Ki.

"May I present Miss Opal Hayes, Jessie. Opal, Miss Jessica Starbuck."

"How do you do?" Jessie said.

"I'm very pleased to meet you, Miss Starbuck." As Opal pronounced the name, her eyes suddenly widened. "Starbuck," she repeated in an almost reverent tone of

45

voice. "You're not *the* Jessica Starbuck? Alex Starbuck's daughter?"

Jessie nodded.

"Oh, I've heard ever so much about you and your family, Miss Starbuck," Opal enthused. "But I never thought I'd have the privilege of meeting you in person."

"Let's sit down so that we can continue this conversation in comfort and relative privacy," Ki suggested. He indicated with a curt gesture the men and women who had gathered while Ki was still holding on to Keane. All of whom were either talking with the conductor or still gawking at Ki, some with admiration, some with awe.

They returned to the first class coach where Ki sat down opposite the women. "I'll take that," he said and held out his hand to Opal.

"Take—" She stared blankly at him. "Oh, this." She handed him Keane's hideout derringer. "I had quite forgotten I had it."

Opal then proceeded to tell Jessie all about what had just happened, glancing occasionally at Ki as she told of his role in "saving me from that terrible man." Then, to Ki, "What was it you called him? A 'board thrower'?"

"A broad thrower," Ki corrected. "Many people refer to playing cards as 'broads.' Professional gamblers, even casual players, are, therefore, frequently called either 'broad throwers' or 'broad pitchers' because they throw or pitch the cards."

"You said that gambling on Texas and Pacific trains was illegal," Opal reminded Ki. "I hadn't known that. My goodness, to think that I was performing a criminal act every time I played with Matthew—with that awful man. Me, the daughter of a law officer! Papa would be shamed six ways to Sunday were he to find out about my misbehavior."

"Your father's a law officer?" Jessie said. "Where, may I ask?"

"In El Paso. He's the marshal there. Marshal Buck Hayes. Papa's real name is James, but everyone calls him Buck."

"Then you, I take it," Ki said, "are traveling to El Paso as Jessie and I are."

"Yes. I've just finished the term at Miss Altamount's School for Young Ladies in Philadelphia, and I'm on my way to visit for a spell with papa."

"I've always been fascinated by the law and the men who enforce it," Ki said. "Perhaps you would introduce me to your father."

"Oh, I would love to introduce you to papa. I know he would love to meet you. Especially after I tell him how you came so gallantly to my rescue."

Ki refused to acknowledge the knowing look Jessie was giving him. He kept his attention centered on Opal.

"Perhaps it would be a good idea if you didn't tell your father that you were playing three-card monte with Keane," Ki said.

"He'll pretend to be shocked, of course," Opal mused. "But he won't be. Not really. He knows full well I've got an independent mind and a venturesome spirit." As she spoke her last sentence Opal stared straight at Ki. She added, "He blames himself for having let me, as he likes to put it, 'grow up wild with the yearlings.' That's why he sent me away to Miss Altamount's. 'To soften all your rough edges,' he said once. 'To tame the tiger,' he said another time, as I recall."

"Indian Junction!" bellowed the conductor from the far end of the car, pronouncing the first word "Injun." "We'll be stopping here longer than is customary, ladies and gents. We usually lay over only fifteen minutes—just long enough for those so inclined to wet their whistles or grab a

47

bite to eat. But there's a coach full of emigrants that's been sitting on a siding at the Junction for nigh onto two days and we're going to hook them up with us. It'll take some time."

When the conductor had gone, Ki rose. "Shall we get something to eat, ladies?"

"You and Opal go ahead, Ki," Jessie said. "I'll walk about a little to stretch my legs and join you both later."

As Opal left her seat and started down the aisle, Jessie beckoned to Ki. He bent down to hear her whisper in his ear, "I suggest you watch your step. In my opinion, that tiger isn't altogether tamed yet."

Ki couldn't help himself. He guffawed at Jessie's totally unexpected comment. Then he grinned and told her, *"Tame* tigers never did interest me very much."

Chapter 4

Ki, with Opal on his arm, entered the Harvey House Dining Hall that adjoined the train depot and was almost deafened by the din within the cavernous room.

He found a place at the service counter for himself and Opal by firmly forcing his way between two men. When Opal had taken a seat on one of the cloth-covered stools at the counter, he sat down beside her and, shouting to make himself heard asked her what she wanted to order. From a blackboard on which had been chalked the names of the food and beverage items being offered for sale, she chose a roast beef sandwich, coffee, and a piece of angel food cake. Ki managed to convey her order and his own—a ham sandwich and tea—to one of the Harvey girls serving behind the three-sided counter. By the time their orders were placed before them some minutes later, the noise inside the dining hall had diminished greatly as the train passengers concentrated on devouring the food and drink they had been served.

"I think I should like to be a Harvey Girl," Opal volunteered as she watched the women who were all dressed exactly alike in long black dresses with sleeves to the elbow over which they wore spotless white aprons that completely covered their upper torsos and reached to their ankles.

"Why?" Ki asked, before biting into his ham sandwich, which turned out to be too salty for his taste.

"Oh, one would get to meet so many interesting men," Opal replied, glancing about the room that was packed mostly with men.

"Some of them might turn out to be not very gentlemanly," Ki pointed out. "Your Mr. Matthew Keane wasn't."

"I can take care of myself," Opal declared somewhat huffily. Then, contritely, she added, "Aren't I the awful liar though? I didn't take care of myself very well at all where he was concerned. I am eternally in your debt, Ki."

They finished eating, and Ki paid for their meals. Then they made their way outside where Ki found the conductor of their train standing in the midst of a sea of horse-drawn carriages. He inquired concerning the time of their departure. The conductor advised him that they would not be leaving for another hour at least. There was, according to the conductor, some damage to the track on the siding where the emigrants' coach was resting. Until it was repaired the emigrants' car could not be connected to the Texas and Pacific train.

"Would you like to get out of the sun?" Ki asked Opal. "It's becoming rather hot."

"Shall we go inside the depot?"

"I was thinking you might want to freshen up. Rest your eyes, perhaps. There is a hotel just down the block." He pointed to the building that had a sign above its entrance which read: DROVER'S REST.

"That sounds wonderful."

And it was wonderful, Ki found, because the moment

50

they were inside the hotel room with the door closed behind them, Opal came eagerly into his arms. He was instantly erect again, as he had been when he first saw her singing in the train's parlor car.

"I knew when I first saw you that you wanted me," Opal murmured. She planted hot kisses on his lips, his face, his neck. "Did you know that I wanted you just as much?"

"No," Ki managed to murmur between two of Opal's passionate assaults on his lips.

"Well, that's not surprising, is it?" she asked, stepping back and placing her hands on Ki's shoulders. "I mean, where women are concerned, desire is not obviously manifested as it is with men—as it was with you in the parlor coach."

Before Ki could say anything, Opal cried, "Why, you're blushing! Have I embarrassed you?"

He didn't answer her question; he kissed her instead.

Then he helped her undress.

Then he undressed in what must have been, he thought, record time.

She came to him, walking through the pile of clothes that littered the floor between them, and clasped his shaft in her hot hand. It sprouted beyond her hand's confines. She covered it completely with her other hand.

Ki throbbed in her hands. He threw back his head and moaned as she ran her hands—her flickering fingers—up and down his body, touching him here, touching him there —his nipples, his navel, his inner thighs, his buttocks.

Then, suddenly, nothing. He opened his eyes. For an instant, he thought she was gone. But she was not. She was on her knees before him. Looking down, he watched his rock-hard erection slip, inch by slow inch, between her lips and deep within her mouth until her lips were pressed up against his pubic hair.

She paused a moment, holding him inside her mouth

51

while her fingers glided up and down his legs and sent chills coursing through his body. Then she began to suck.

It began with a rising heat that Ki found pleasant. The heat soon became fiery. It threatened to consume him in flames of ecstasy.

The world went away. Reality was, for Ki, centered now in his loins, which seemed about to burst with pleasure. He thrust himself into Opal and she took him willingly. She made wet, sucking sounds as he placed his hands behind her head and interlocked his fingers. Holding her head steady, he moved wildly, feeling himself close to a climax. To prevent himself from coming, he let go of Opal and withdrew from her mouth. Taking her by the hand, he helped her to her feet and led her to the bed.

"No," she said.

"What's wrong?"

"I want to be on top. Is that all right? Or would you prefer—"

"That's fine." Ki lay down on his back on the bed, and Opal straddled him. His shaft was still stiff and pointing toward his chin. She grasped it, positioned herself, and deftly placed him within her.

Ki's back arched as if trying to ram his rock-hard member even farther inside her.

Opal began to rise and fall upon him, and because of her earlier ministrations, Ki came within less than a minute, his climax coinciding with hers.

Opal sat on his thighs and stared into his eyes. Seconds passed during which Ki fondled her breasts with both hands.

"It's still hard," she whispered. "I thought you might be—you know, finished for now."

But Ki was far from finished. Two orgasms later for him and the same number for Opal, both were spent but satisfied.

Their passion drained, both of them became aware of the passage of time. They dressed quickly and left the hotel. Back at the depot, they boarded the train to find Jessie in her seat, reading a copy of Indian Junction's newspaper. She looked up as they joined her.

"Did you have something to eat?" Ki asked her as he sat down beside her. Opal took the seat opposite them.

"Yes. An omelette with chili peppers. It was quite good. And you two?"

"I ate," Opal said, "and everything was simply delicious." She glanced at Ki.

Slyly, he thought. Was she referring to eating his——. He had no time to speculate further. At that precise moment, the conductor made his way down the aisle. He glanced at Opal in passing, hesitated a moment, and then retraced his steps and stood, hands on hips, facing her.

"May I see your ticket, Miss?"

Opal opened her reticle, found her ticket and handed it to him.

"Second class passenger," he muttered. "I thought I recognized you." He righteously clucked his tongue against the roof of his mouth. *"Second* class passengers are not allowed out of the *second* class coach."

"I beg your pardon, I'm sure," Opal said haughtily. "If you'll excuse me, Ki, Miss Starbuck."

She rose to her feet, swung her reticule so that it struck the conductor's protruding paunch. Deliberately, Ki was convinced. Then she flounced down the aisle and on into the second class coach.

The conductor followed her. Ki hoped they wouldn't come to blows over Opal's trespassing.

"I looked for you in the dining hall and around the depot," Jessie said to him as she turned a page of the Indian Junction newspaper she had been reading. "I didn't see you. Or Miss Hayes either, for that matter."

"We—"

Before Ki could say anything more, Jessie cried out.

"What is it?" he asked her, startled by her exclamation. "What's the matter?"

Jessie's mouth moved but no words came. She pointed at the paper, her eyes glued to it.

Ki leaned closer to her.

She was pointing at an obituary notice, Brent Latrobe's obituary notice.

But what, he wondered, had so startled her? She shouldn't have been surprised to see such a notice, he reasoned, because Brent Latrobe was a prominent figure in the state of Texas. Notice of his death would be taken by newspapers from El Paso to Fort Worth to Austin, the state capitol.

"Ki, it says here that Brent Latrobe committed suicide."

Jessie handed the newspaper to Ki who proceeded to read the obituary notice.

One of our fair state's most progressive and beloved citizens has passed from among us. Mr. Brent Latrobe, businessman, cultural leader, and friend of both the mighty and the meek, was found dead in his office by Marshal James "Buck" Hayes in El Paso. Marshal Hayes reported that Mr. Latrobe was found hanging from a closet door in his office and was dead at the time of discovery.

The coroner confirms that Mr. Latrobe died by his own hand. The cause of death is listed as a broken neck.

Relatives and friends may view the body in El Paso and offer their condolences to Mr. Latrobe's widow, Theresa, who survives him. Funeral services are scheduled for Tuesday morning. Burial will be in El Paso's Gate of Heaven Cemetery.

Tuesday, Ki thought. That's tomorrow. He glanced at Jessie.

"I can't believe it," she said softly. "I just can't believe that Brent would commit suicide."

"Life does strange things to people," Ki remarked. "It changes them sometimes. Mr. Latrobe must have had a reason for what he did. Maybe Mrs. Latrobe will be able to explain that reason to us."

Jessie nodded absently, as she tried to absorb the shocking information she had been given about the cause of her friend's death.

At nineteen minutes after one o'clock the following afternoon, the Texas and Pacific train pulled into the depot of El Paso, exactly twenty-two minutes late.

As Ki stepped down from the train behind Jessie with their luggage in his hands, he saw Opal leave the second class coach and come running toward him along the wooden platform. He set down the bags he was carrying, ready to embrace her when she reached him.

She ran right past him and into the arms of another man standing some distance beyond Ki, a man wearing a tin star pinned to his vest.

"Are you coming?" Jessie asked him as he stood watching Opal and the lawman hug one another as if they would never let go.

"I'm coming," Ki said in answer to Jessie's question. He picked up their bags again and started to follow Jessie down the platform.

He halted at the sound of Opal calling his name. Turning, he saw her leading the lawman toward him.

"Ki, this is my father, Marshal Buck Hayes," she said when the pair reached Ki. "Papa, this is the man I just told you about."

"Howdy," Hayes said, offering his hand to Ki.

Ki put down the bags, and the two men shook hands.

Hayes said, "Opal just told me about how you saved her from the clutches of that gambling man she got herself mixed up with in Omaha. I'm much obliged to you, sir."

"Oh, Miss Starbuck!" Opal called out. She beckoned to Jessie who had halted and was standing some distance away.

Jessie, in response to Opal's summons, joined the group and was introduced to Marshal Hayes.

"It's a true honor to meet you, Miss Starbuck," said Hayes, doffing his Stetson. "I've heard nothing but good things about your father. You too, for that matter."

"It's very kind of you to say so, Marshal."

"What brings you to our fair city, Miss Starbuck?"

"Ki and I have come to pay our last respects to Brent Latrobe."

"Oh, you knew Mr. Latrobe, did you?"

"Since I was a child, yes. He and his wife—his widow now—have been my friends for many years."

"A sad thing. A very sad thing indeed, Mr. Latrobe's passing."

"During the trip here," Jessie said, "I read in a newspaper that Mr. Latrobe committed suicide and that you were the one who found him, Marshal. Is that account of the matter correct?"

"Yes, I'm sorry to say it is," Hayes answered, twisting his hat in his hands.

"Where did you find him?"

"In his office, Miss Starbuck. I was making my rounds and I saw a lamp burning in his office. Now, I knew that Mr. Latrobe sometimes worked late—he was a hard worker, Mr. Latrobe was—but it was past three a.m. when I saw the lamp still alight in his office. I knocked on the door to see if he was in there, to see if he was all right. I didn't get any answer. I don't mind telling you that made me a bit skittish."

"You saw no one in the office?" Ki inquired.

"Nope. Not a soul."

"What did you do?" Jessie asked.

"I pounded on the door real hard. But I couldn't raise anybody. I tried the door and damn—excuse me, ladies— if it wasn't unlocked. So in I went without wasting another minute."

"You found Mr. Latrobe inside," Ki said. "Can you tell us about that?"

"He was in this little cubbyhole of a room he had in the back of his office. It was a washroom of sorts with a slop jar—excuse me again, ladies."

"Go on, Marshal," Jessie urged.

"There he was a hangin' like a steer in a slaughterhouse. What he'd done was, he'd tied a rope around the outside doorknob of the door to the washroom and then he'd looped the rope over the top of the door, stepped up on a footstool, put the noose he'd fashioned around his neck, and stepped off of the footstool into thin air."

"What did you do after you found him?" Ki asked.

"I hightailed it out of the office to rouse our coroner. I rousted him out of a warm bed and into his duds. The two of us, we drove to Mr. Latrobe's office where we cut him down and loaded him onto the wagon and hauled him back to the coroner's place where we laid him out."

"What did the coroner say was the cause of death?" Ki asked.

"Broken neck," Hayes replied.

"Must we talk of such terrible things?" Opal asked, grimacing.

Her father patted her comfortingly on the shoulder. "Death's an unfortunate fact of life, my precious."

Opal made another face.

Jessie said, "Was there anything suspicious about the circumstances surrounding Mr. Latrobe's death in your opinion, Marshal?"

"Suspicious? No, ma'am, I can't say there was anything suspicious about it."

"The unlocked office door?" Ki prodded.

"Now that's not the sort of thing you'd call suspicious," said Hayes, giving Ki an appraising glance. "Not when you take into account two things."

"What two things are you referring to, Marshal?" Jessie asked.

Hayes held up an index finger. "One, this is a safe town. It's not unusual for folk to leave their doors unlocked at all hours of the day or night whether they're home or out gallivanting somewheres." His middle finger sprang up beside his index finger. "Two, Mr. Latrobe was a forgetful sort of fellow. Many's the time I've seen him walking in the rain on account of how he forgot his umbrella. Or wearing two different colored shoes on account of he'd taken one from one pair and the other from another pair altogether. Either one of those two things"—Hayes waggled his two fingers—"could have accounted for him having left his office door unlocked."

"I see," Jessie said. "Thank you, Marshal, for talking to us."

"You'll be at the burying tomorrow, will you?" Hayes asked, his glance flicking from Jessie to Ki and back again. When Jessie nodded, he smiled. "Be seeing you there then."

"Good day, Marshal," Jessie said and turned away.

Before following her, Ki turned to Opal and said, "I hope to see you again, Miss Hayes."

"In that case," Opal said, "I'll come to the burial with papa."

Ki nodded and followed Jessie who was making her

way around to the front of the depot where a number of wagons and carriages of various kinds were parked.

"I don't see anyone who looks like they might have come to pick us up," Jessie remarked as Ki caught up with her. "I hope Tess got the telegraph message I sent telling her the time of our arrival. If no one does come, we can rent a wagon at the livery stable."

Ki raised a hand to shield his eyes from the blazing sun and surveyed the area. He studied the elegant two-seat carriage with the extension roof made of black rubber that was racing down a side street, its driver lashing the team of two horses that was pulling the vehicle as he headed for the depot.

"That one must be the one we want," he said as the carriage came closer. He was able to make out the Double L insignia inlaid in brass on the carriage's dash, the insignia that was, Jessie had told him, the brand Brent Latrobe placed on all of his and Tess's stock.

Jessie's eyes were on the driver of the carriage as he braked in front of the depot.

He was a tall man with broad shoulders and narrow hips. His eyes were the color of walnuts in contrast to his hair, which was the color of cornsilk. His face was ruggedly handsome and deeply tanned. His hands were long-fingered and appeared strong.

He was wearing worn and faded jeans tucked into work boots. His blue cotton shirt bore sweat marks on the back and under the arms. The ends of the red bandanna he wore tied around his neck fluttered in the faint breeze. On his head was a rumpled black felt hat, also sweat-stained.

He was staring at Jessie with a penetrating gaze that seemed to freeze her in her tracks. She met it, but with some difficulty. She felt that the driver of the carriage was somehow reading all her secret thoughts and desires. That he knew everything there was to know about her. That he

59

knew she found him attractive. That she had been wondering what it would be like to be touched by those strong hands of his, to be kissed by his thin, yet decidedly sensuous, lips. It was only with great effort that Jessie did not surrender to the impulse to look away from this stranger with the disconcerting gaze.

He broke the eye contact when he rose and stepped gracefully down from the front seat after wrapping the team's reins around the brake handle.

He stopped a few feet from where Jessie and Ki were standing, his weight balanced on his slightly spread legs, his hand slowly rising to touch the brim of his battered hat.

"I'm sorry I'm late, Miss Starbuck. Didn't mean to keep you and your friend waiting. But one of the carriage's shafts split on the way here and I had to tie it up as best I could with some strips of rawhide. I reckon it'll hold till we get back to the ranch where I can replace it."

"Have we met before?" Jessie asked, knowing they hadn't, but wondering how this man knew who she was when there were a number of other women at the depot, many of them obviously waiting, as she and Ki had been, for someone to meet them.

"No, we've never met before," the man replied.

"Then how did you—"

"Know who you were?" He smiled, his eyes dancing, crow's feet crinkling at their corners. "Mrs. Latrobe told me I wouldn't be able to miss you. She said, 'Cass, you just look for the most beautiful woman at the depot. That'll be Jessie Starbuck.'"

Jessie was blushing as she introduced Ki.

"Names's Cass Henderson," the carriage driver said. He shook hands with Ki and then helped Jessie climb into the rear seat of the carriage.

Ki, after placing their luggage beside Cass in the front seat, took his place beside her.

Cass climbed back into the front seat, picked up the reins, released the brake, and clucked the team into motion.

"Do you work for Mr.—for Mrs. Latrobe, Mr. Henderson?" Jessie inquired, keenly aware of the aura of raw sexuality that seemed to emanate from Cass.

"Yes, ma'am, I do and have done for the past two, nearly three years now. Started as a wrangler. Now I'm ranch foreman."

The information was given with no sense of braggadocio, Jessie noted. The man had simply stated facts.

"How is Tess—Mrs. Latrobe—holding up?" Jessie asked.

"About as well as can be expected," Cass answered, lightly slapping the rumps of the team with the reins. "She's shed her share of tears, and I can't blame her for that. Mr. Latrobe—his loss is a bad-hurting thing. Women it sets to weeping. Men it hardens like winter does the ground. It'll take some time for her hurting to heal."

They passed over a stretch of low-lying soggy ground indicative of a recent rain. Jessie drew back toward Ki, but the gracefully curved fenders over the carriage's rear wheels prevented her from being splashed with mud.

Later, when they arrived at the ranch, there were many carriages and a few wagons parked in front of the building.

Cass drew rein, bringing the team to a halt in front of the door. When Ki had helped Jessie down from the carriage, Cass touched the brim of his hat to her and told her that he would bring the luggage in through the back door.

Jessie and Ki entered the house through the wide open front door. The foyer was filled with men and women and a few children, all of them dressed somberly, most of them in black.

In the large common room, they found more people

61

conversing in low tones. The deceased lay in his pine coffin, which rested on two sawhorses at one end of the room. Near the coffin, Tess Latrobe sat in a high-backed chair, her hands clasped together, her head nodding politely as mourners, after viewing the deceased, bent to offer her their condolences.

Jessie, with Ki at her side, made her way through the crowd toward the coffin that contained the mortal remains of Brent Latrobe. When they reached it, they bowed their heads, each of them silently bidding goodbye to the man they had known and, in Jessie's case, loved.

Jessie then raised her head and stared down at Brent Latrobe who looked, in death, like the shadow of the man she had known in life. Someone—probably the coroner— had attempted to give him a semblance of life by powdering his face and placing a touch of rouge on his cheeks and lips.

Her eyes strayed to his neck, but she could see no sign of rope marks because of the fluffy flowered ascot that covered most of Latrobe's neck. An attempt on the part of the coroner, she supposed, to spare the feelings of those viewing the remains by hiding any grim sign of how Latrobe had died.

Latrobe, in death, was still a solidly built man but his solidity was now like a facade that hid a terrible emptiness. His unruly shock of white hair crowned a head that now seemed somehow shrunken.

Jessie forced herself to face the fact that she would never again hear Brent Latrobe's vibrant laugh or feel the touch of his large but surprisingly gentle hands. She reached out and tenderly touched those cold white hands that were so neatly folded in an imitation of serenity. Then, fighting back her tears, she turned to greet Tess.

The widow had been watching her intently from the moment Jessie had entered the room. Now Tess rose from her chair, unclasped her hands, and opened her arms wide. Jessie moved into Tess's warm embrace and found herself being comforted by her dead friend's widow.

Finally, Jessie found her voice. "Tess, I can't tell you how sorry I am."

Tess patted Jessie's shoulder. "I know, dear, I know. Thank you so much for coming. I have to talk to you, Jessie. Tonight. When everyone else has gone."

"Tess, you remember Ki, don't you?"

"Of course," Tess said. She shook hands with Ki who told her how deeply he regretted her loss.

"I trust that you and Jessie," Tess said to him, "will be able to help me."

"We will do anything we can to help, Mrs. Latrobe," Ki assured her.

"Just tell us what you want us to do, Tess," Jessie said. "What it is you need."

"They are saying that Brent committed suicide."

Jessie was about to say that she had spoken to Marshal Hayes and read in the Indian Junction newspaper that such was the case, but Tess gave her no chance to speak.

"I don't believe it," Tess said firmly. "I want you two, if you will, to find out the true circumstances surrounding my husband's death."

"The *true* circumstances?" an obviously puzzled Ki asked.

"Yes. As I've just said, I don't for one minute believe Brent took his own life. I want you two to find out what really caused my husband's death."

Jessie and Ki exchanged glances. Troubled glances.

Chapter 5

Late that night, after the last of the mourners had gone, Tess Latrobe sent the servants to bed and then led Jessie and Ki into the huge kitchen of the ranch house where she proceeded to make coffee.

Jessie protested, pointing out that Tess looked tired—tired to the bone, she thought, but did not say so—and that she would gladly make the coffee while Tess rested.

But Tess would not hear of it. "I *am* tired," she admitted, "but I would rather be doing something, anything, than be forced to sit as I have been for almost the entire past two days and have things done for me."

She fired up the cast iron stove and put the pot of coffee on to boil. "Oh, I know everyone means well," she sighed. "But you know me, Jessie. I cannot abide having things done for me or being treated as if I were an invalid, which I decidedly am not."

Jessie sat across from Ki at the large wooden table in the center of the kitchen. She waited until Tess had poured the coffee and had seated herself at the table before venturing to bring up the matter that was weighing on her mind.

"Tess," she began with a sense of trepidation, as one does when around someone inclined to become easily upset, "what did you mean when you said earlier tonight that you didn't believe Brent had taken his own life?"

Tess pursed her lips. "He would never have done such a thing."

Jessie glanced at Ki. He picked up one her non-verbal cue and turned to Tess and said, "We happened to meet Marshal Hayes at the depot in town when we arrived, Mrs. Latrobe. He told us that Mr. Latrobe had"—Ki knew there was no way to put it delicately so he plunged on—"hung himself in his office."

Tess said nothing. When she simply stared at Ki as if she had not understood a word he had said, Jessie ventured, "That's also what it said in the Indian Junction newspaper that I read on the way here, Tess."

When Tess finally spoke, her voice was firm. "I don't care what Buck Hayes or any newspaper says. Brent did not commit suicide."

She won't accept reality, Jessie thought, staring with heartfelt sympathy at Tess as the woman sat with her hands encircling her coffee cup, as if for warmth. She can't face the truth. It's just too terrible. So she denies it and makes up her own version of reality, one she can more comfortably live with.

"Our anniversary was—is—what is the right word now that Brent is dead?"

For a moment, Jessie thought Tess was confused, that she was rambling. But then the older woman continued, "Brent and I would have been married twenty-four years this Thursday."

Ki, his eyes on Tess, wondered where the remark was leading, if anywhere. Was it merely the sentimental musing of a bereaved woman?

Tess continued, "Brent told me he had a special surprise

for me for our anniversary. He told me that a week ago. But he didn't tell me what the surprise was because, he said, it wouldn't be a surprise if he told me."

A fond smile drifted across Tess's face and then was gone. "'There's no use badgering me, old girl,' he said, 'I won't tell you what it is. But I will tell you this. You're going to love it.'" Tess's smile returned to soften her features. "As you know, Jessie, Brent could be positively infuriating at times."

"I know. I remember the time you two were visiting us at our ranch, and it was my birthday. Brent would not, absolutely *would not,* give me my birthday present before what he called 'the appointed day.' I was furious with him at the time."

"Neither of us," Tess said to Jessie, "ever could stand suspense very well." She sipped from her cup. "You're undoubtedly wondering why I bring up the matter of my anniversary present. No, it's not the nattering of an old woman deranged by grief."

"We didn't think that for a minute," Ki said gently.

Tess reached out and patted his hand. "I brought it up only to show you that Brent had no intention of committing suicide. On the contrary, he was as full of life as ever and positively gloating over the surprise, whatever it might have been, that he planned to give me on our anniversary next Thursday."

"Jessie, you know Brent. You must realize that he couldn't have committed suicide."

Jessie desperately wanted to be able to say that, yes, she knew such a thing was impossible. But there was no way she could say it, even though she wouldn't be the first person in the world to tell a mild lie to save someone from suffering.

She drew a breath and said, "There may have been

66

things going on in his life, Tess, that you didn't know about. It may be that—"

"Oh, there were things going on in Brent's life that I didn't know about," Tess volunteered without looking directly at either Jessie or Ki. "Things that I didn't find out about until after Brent was dead."

"What things, Mrs. Latrobe?" Ki asked, not sure if he was overstepping the bounds of good taste, but he wanted to clear up the matter that seemed to be clouding the air in the kitchen.

"I am at the moment practically a pauper."

Jessie's sudden intake of breath, a sign of her shocked reaction to Tess's words, was loud in the quiet kitchen.

"Can you explain what you mean, Mrs. Latrobe?" Ki asked.

"That won't be necessary," Jessie quickly interpolated, giving Ki a frown. "It's none of our business."

"Ki has every right to ask the question, Jessie," Tess insisted. "He is only trying to help me and to help me he has to understand—everything."

Ki emptied his cup.

Jessie got up and refilled it. Tess refused any more coffee, saying her nerves were bad enough without inflicting more coffee on them.

"Let me explain what I meant earlier when I said I am now almost poverty-stricken. When news of Brent's death got around—and it spread like wildfire, I can tell you—I received a visit, ostensibly of condolence, from a local businessman named Arthur Reese." She harrumphed. "Visit of condolence, indeed! Vultures don't pay visits of condolence.

"But let me get on with this. Arthur informed me that Brent had borrowed money from him recently on two occasions. A great deal of money, he gave me to understand.

A total of one hundred and forty-five thousand dollars, actually."

Jessie, thunderstruck, didn't speak. Nor did Ki.

Tess, seeing the shocked expression on both their faces, nodded grimly. "According to Arthur, there are also others to whom Brent was in debt before his death. One of them is the most successful banker in El Paso, a man by the name of Addison Chaney. Arthur advised me of the fact that Brent signed a mortgage on this homestead in exchange for another substantial loan from Chaney's bank, the El Paso Trust. Then there is Lon Curlew, a stockman with considerable holdings here in southwestern Texas. Arthur advises me that Brent also borrowed heavily from Curlew with the unhappy result that Curlew holds a chattel mortgage on all Latrobe cattle."

"What you're telling me," Jessie said in a strained voice, "is hard to believe. Brent was always so careful about the way he used credit. I can't believe he would overextend himself in such a fashion."

"Perhaps there had been business reverses that your husband didn't tell you about, Mrs. Latrobe," Kit remarked.

"I don't believe there were," Tess said quickly. "Brent would have told me about them. He always told me everything. He treated me as an equal partner. That's what our brand represents—our partnership and joint ownership of everything. The Double L brand. It stands for both of us— Brent Latrobe and Theresa Latrobe. Brent frequently asked my advice on business matters and I was always glad to give it. Ours was a true partnership, even if we didn't always see eye to eye on everything. I kept the books and he tended to everything else."

"You kept the books," Ki repeated thoughtfully. "That surprises and, quite frankly, puzzles me, Mrs. Latrobe."

"I'm afraid I don't understand, Ki," Tess said, her brow wrinkling.

"If you kept the books, how is it that you weren't aware of your husband's growing indebtedness?" Ki inquired as gently as he could.

"But that's just it, you see," Tess exclaimed. "There is nothing in the books to indicate that he had borrowed money from Arthur Reese or from anyone else, for that matter."

"You mean to say that Brent hid his financial problems from you?" Jessie asked.

"Yes," Tess answered in a barely audible voice. "He never did that before, never once."

A thought Jessie didn't want to think crossed her mind. She wondered if the same thought had already crossed Tess's mind. She had to mention it, cruel though it might be to do so. "Tess, is it possible that Brent was so overwhelmed with business problems—with the immense indebtedness he had incurred with Reese, Chaney, Curlew, and possibly others—that he took his own life?"

Tess tapped the fingers of her right hand on the table for a moment before answering. "No, I don't think that's what happened." She looked up at Jessie. "You know Brent. You know he was a fighter. You know, as I do, that he wouldn't give up, that he'd fight his battles through to the bitter end. He wouldn't—surrender—like that. He wouldn't kill himself, no, he wouldn't, he . . . ."

Tess folded her arms on the table top, lowered her head to them, and dissolved in tears and shoulder-shaking sobs.

After Tess had gone to bed, Jessie sat with Ki in the kitchen. The coffee in their cups had grown cold.

"We've got to do something to help Tess," Jessie said, as if she were talking to herself.

"What do you want to do?" Ki asked.

"I don't know. To tell you the truth, I'm not sure there is anything we can do. I mean what Tess believes—that her husband didn't commit suicide—flies in the face of the facts. What can we do to help her when she seems to be living in a kind of dream world where she has twisted reality to fit not the facts, but what she wants—or perhaps needs—to believe about the circumstances of her husband's death?

"Ki, I don't see how we can help Tess. But I can't just abandon the woman under the circumstances. She was almost as much a friend to me as Brent was."

"We could talk to people," Ki suggested. "See what they have to tell us about Mr. Latrobe—especially anything they might have noticed in the days preceding his death that might help us help Tess."

Jessie leaned back in her chair and wearily rubbed her closed eyes with the tips of her fingers. "Let's do that. It probably won't do us—or Tess—any good, but at least it will show her that we're trying to help her, that we don't think she's . . ."

As Jessie's voice trailed away, Ki said, "You've been thinking the same thing that I've been thinking." When Jessie glanced at him, he added, "You've been thinking that grief might have temporarily unhinged Mrs. Latrobe and kept her from thinking straight."

"It shames me to admit it but, yes, Ki, that is exactly what I've been thinking."

"We could talk to Arthur Reese. We could ask to see the records of Mr. Latrobe's indebtedness to him."

"That's a good idea. Let's go into town tomorrow after the funeral service and burial. While we're at it, we could also talk to the others who, according to Tess, have liens on the Latrobe holdings."

"The banker, Addison Chaney," Ki said. "And the stockman, Lon Curlew."

Jessie nodded. "There's one other person I want to talk to as well."

"Who's that?"

"The coroner. I want to know what he can tell us about his examination of Brent's body after he and Marshal Hayes cut it down and took it to his mortuary."

Jessie, Ki, and Tess stood side by side in front of the open grave in Gate of Heaven Cemetery early the next morning, Jessie to Tess's right, Ki to her left.

The preacher made his slow and solemn way to the head of the gaping grave and stood there, bible in hand. The six pall bearers slid ropes beneath the pine coffin that had been nailed shut. With three of them on one side of the grave and three on the other, they gripped the ropes and lowered Brent Latrobe into the earth.

Jessie, holding Tess's arm, felt the woman tremble. She tightened her grip on the widow's arm and Tess's trembling gradually subsided.

"Oh that my words were now written! Oh that they were printed in a book!" intoned the preacher, reading from the Book of Job. "That they were graven with an iron pen and lead in the rock for ever!"

Jessie became aware of the soft whispery weeping that emanated from several black-clad women who stood sorrowfully among the circle of people surrounding the grave. She fought back her own tears.

The preacher's voice rose to a pious roar as he lifted his eyes to the skies and declaimed, "For I know that my Redeemer liveth, and that He shall stand at the latter day upon the earth: And though after my skin worms destroy this body, yet in my flesh shall I see God: Whom I shall see for myself, and mine eyes shall behold, and not another; though my reins be consumed within me."

As the preacher's voice droned on, occasionally rising

to something just short of a rapturous shriek, Jessie scanned the crowd. It was mostly composed of men. There were women, of course, but the men outnumbered them.

Cass Henderson was there, attired in a black suit, white shirt, and black string tie. As her gaze lingered on the ranch foreman, she thought that he looked like a man full of vibrant energy barely held in check. She could imagine him at work: quick, cool, efficient. She could imagine him in bed with a woman: strong, lusty, insatiable. He noticed her studying him and as he did his gaze held her. She refused to look away from him. She refused to drop her eyes. She felt something pass between them, a not so secret message. He was, as she interpreted the message his riveting eyes were sending her, as captivated by her as she was by him.

The men clustered around Cass were all Latrobe ranch hands, she supposed, since they all had that rough-hewn look about them. Only when one of them spoke to Cass, did he take his eyes away from Jessie.

The only other man present that she knew was Marshal Buck Hayes who stood with his daughter, Opal, on the opposite side of the grave. He was twisting his hat in his hands as he had done the day before when Jessie had first met him at the depot.

A nervous man, she thought. Edgy. She noted the way his eyes strayed here and there, lighting on the face of a man in a pearl gray flannel suit and then quickly away when the man's keen eyes met his. They roamed next to the flush face of a rotund man with a bright gold watch-chain looping across his embroidered vest. This man stood with his hands piously folded in front of him looking morosely down into the grave where the pine coffin rested.

Buck Hayes' eyes moved on to yet another man who was standing with the aid of a cane on the far side of Ki. The man was completely bald and his ears stuck out like the handles of a jug. He too was well-dressed and looked decidedly prosperous. The marshal's eyes dropped down toward the grave and then quickly closed.

He doesn't want to look into the grave, Jessie thought. The sight of the coffin unnerves him. Not unusual, not at all unusual. Most people have trouble coming to terms with the inescapable fact of their own mortality. And most of us, Jessie thought, don't like funerals or looking down into gaping graves because such sights only serve to confirm the fact that inevitably we will one day share the fate of the one inside the coffin. No wonder Buck Hayes' eyes looked everywhere but at the grave and what it contained.

The preacher, no longer quoting from his bible, but saying something in mellifluous tones about meeting the dearly departed again in the sweet by and by, finally brought the burial service to an end.

Tess stood her ground and spoke briefly with the many mourners who came up to her to express their sorrow and to wish her well in the days ahead. The days she would spend alone now that her beloved was gone.

The man in the pearl gray flannel suit approached Tess.

Jessie heard Tess call the man "Arthur."

"Was that Arthur Reese?" Jessie whispered to Tess as the man moved away toward his carriage.

Tess nodded. "And that," she said, with a nod in the direction of the man with the florid face and embroidered vest whom Jessie had seen Buck Hayes looking at earlier, "is Addison Chaney, the banker. Over there,"—another nod in the opposite direction, this time to the bald man who was limping away from the grave with the help of his cane,—"that's Lon Curlew."

Jessie watched Curlew climb into his carriage. So there they are, she thought, the three of them who are now the owners of just about every cow and chair and outbuilding that once belonged to Brent and Tess Latrobe. A terrible sense of loss swept over her as the immensity of the debacle Brent Latrobe had brought upon himself and his wife became painfully clear to her.

Jessie was about to speak to Tess when a tall, heavy set bushy-bearded man emerged from among the crowd of mourners and took Tess's small hand in his large one.

"My dear Tess," he said in a surprisingly soft voice for such a large man, "I want to tell you once again—and I mean this from the bottom of my heart—that I stand ready to do anything I can to help you in this your time of sorrow."

"Thank you, Charles. I know you mean what you say, and I assure you that I will indeed call on you should I find myself in need of your help. You were always a good friend to Brent and me."

"I remain your good friend, Tess. Don't ever forget that." The man took Tess in his arms and held her close to him for a long moment before releasing her and moving away.

"Everyone has been so kind," Tess sighed. "Oh, I should have introduced you, Jessie. My mind's in a muddle ever since . . . Forgive me, Jessie."

"That's quite all right, Tess."

"That was Charles Tremayne. He's been a good friend to Brent and me over the years."

"Is he a stockman?"

"Well, yes, he is. He's currently vice president of the Cattlemen's Association. But in the past few years his primary interest has been in real estate. He has invested rather heavily in this part of the state and his investments, I understand, have been very profitable for him. He owns some of the richest grazing land in all of Texas, somewhere around half a million acres, I believe. Which is not to mention the town sites he has sold and helped develop."

"I'm so sorry for your trouble, Mrs. Latrobe," said Opal

74

Hayes as she suddenly materialized in front of Tess.

"Thank you, child."

As Opal curtsied and turned to Ki, Jessie said, "It's time to go, Tess. Are you ready?"

"In a moment. I want to say goodbye to Brent first."

Jessie moved away to give Tess privacy, and as she did so Opal moved close to Ki.

Tess walked around the end of the grave to where a honeysuckle vine was climbing the stout trunk of a sycamore tree. She plucked a length of the vine that bore trumpet-shaped yellow blossoms and returned to the grave.

From where Jessie stood, she could see Tess's lips moving, but she was too far away to hear the widow's words.

Then Tess, tears flooding her eyes, dropped the spray of honeysuckle into the grave and blew Brent Latrobe a final farewell kiss.

"I know a place we can go," Opal whispered to Ki with a surreptitious glance at her father, the marshal, who was standing by a surrey watching her.

Ki glanced at the open grave that was already being filled by two men with spades. He heard Opal's seductive words echo in his ears. The dead have had their day, he thought. The living still have theirs.

"You want to?" she asked him. "Go with me, I mean?"

Ki did. "Your father—" he began, but Opal put a finger to his lips and then fled from him.

He watched her run toward her father and then speak earnestly to him.

Jessie appeared at Ki's side. "Are you coming back to the ranch with us?"

"I thought I'd stay and talk to Opal for awhile."

Jessie arched her eyebrows. "Oh?"

Ki gave her a look of sublime innocence.

Smiling at him, Jessie said, "Well, we'll see you later then."

A moment after Jessie had returned to Tess, Opal rejoined Ki.

"I told papa that he should ride home with Mr. Reese and leave the surrey for me. I told him that you and I were going to take a little walk together."

Talk. Walk. Well, Ki thought, call it what you will, it did seem to be the thing that made the world go round.

"There's a creek down that way," Opal said, pointing. "It's just the loveliest place in the whole world. It's got nice grassy ground and in some places the moss is so soft you feel like you're lying on goose down."

So, thought Ki. We'll be lying on moss as soft as goose down. He could feel himself stiffening at the thought.

"There are wildflowers there just as pretty as you please and if we get too hot—"

Ah, thought Ki. Now we come to it.

"—we can take off our shoes and dip our feet in the creek. It's always cool and refreshing, even in August."

It wasn't his feet that Ki was planning on dipping. She took his hand and led him through a stand of high grass, chattering away about how he must think her terrible for wanting to be with him the way they were in the hotel back in Indian Junction when somebody had just died, but after all she was young and so was Ki and they couldn't be expected to deny their youthful natures, could they?

Opal led Ki through a stand of scrub pine interspersed with ocotillo bushes and then across a sandy expanse of ground that eventually gave way to a stand of cedars on the bank of the creek Opal had mentioned.

She led him along its winding course until they came to a kind of grotto through which the creek ambled.

"No one can see us here," she told Ki and kissed him full on the lips, her palms cradling his face.

76

He put his arms around her waist and opened his mouth. His tongue slid between his teeth and then between Opal's. He probed. She took his tongue and sucked on it so hard he feared she might uproot it.

Suddenly, she released him and stepped back. "What are you?" she asked him. "Chinese or something?"

"No, I'm a half-blood. Half-American on my father's side, half-Japanese on my mother's side. Why do you ask?"

"Maybe it's the mix," Opal mused, her left elbow cupped in the palm of her right hand, her left index finger tapping her cheek.

"The mix?" inquired a thoroughly confused Ki.

"You know."

Ki definitely didn't.

"The mix of American and Japanese blood."

Ki still didn't understand what it was she was getting at.

"The American men I've been with," Opal said, "are mostly such gentlemen that it takes a lot of the fun out of it for me. Now, don't get me wrong. I'm not saying you're not a gentleman. You are. But you're something else too. You're wild. You let yourself go. You make a girl feel like there's nothing wrong with wanting to roll in the hay while loving every minute she's doing it, which is what I want to do with you *right now!*"

Ki thought he had never seen anyone move so fast. Opal set a record for stripping herself down to the skin. A record he almost, but not quite, matched.

When they were together on the mossy ground, he plunged into Opal without a moment's hesitation. She seemed, if he had read her right, not to want to waste time with preliminaries.

He was right. She was more than moist; she was wet. And she welcomed him lustily, thrusting her hips up toward him and wrapping both her arms and her legs around his body.

They went at it then, both of them moaning and groaning, both of them overflowing with desire. Finally, both of them climaxed with a blend of sounds: yelps from Opal, a series of guttural grunts from Ki.

He lay there upon her, his hips shuddering in a pale imitation of intercourse, his breath coming in shallow gasps. She tossed her head from side to side and squeezed his still-stiff shaft with the muscles of her hot body.

"It's definitely the mix," Opal muttered through clenched teeth.

"You deserve the biggest share of the credit," Ki murmured, his cheek pressed against hers. "The way you let yourself go, the way you just have at it. . . ."

Opal giggled. "Aren't we awful?"

Ki raised himself up on his elbows and looked down at her. "Awful?"

"Poor Mr. Latrobe is dead and gone and here we are making love like two crazy loons."

"There's nothing crazy about us or what we just did. It's just the way of things."

"Papa was so upset about Mr. Latrobe dying and all. I've never known him—no, don't pull out, please, Ki. Let's just stay like this for awhile longer."

Ki remained where he was, feeling his erection, which had started to soften, begin again to throb.

"I've never known papa to be so upset over anyone's passing before. Why, not even when mama died of the pleurisy did he get so down in the dumps. Maybe it's because he's older now. I guess when a person grows older he tends to be more affected by death than he was when he was young."

Opal's words sparked something in Ki's mind. At first, because he was still so wildly aware of Opal and her arousing sensuality, he couldn't put his finger on what it was she had made him think of. But then it came to him.

"Is your father a good friend of Arthur Reese's?" he asked.

"He is now, I gather, but he wasn't before I went away to school in Philadelphia. Why do you ask?"

"You told me you told your father to ride home with Reese. I figured they must be friends, good friends maybe, if you told him to do that. Otherwise, it would have been an imposition to just up and ask somebody you didn't know very well to take you home."

"Papa is good friends with all the important people in town. Why, Mr. Addison Chaney even offered him a job, he told me."

Addison Chaney, Ki thought. The town banker. "A job?"

"Mr. Chaney asked papa if he would want to be a private guard at Mr. Chaney's bank, but papa told me he said no thank you to Mr. Chaney because he liked being town marshal just fine."

"Does your father—"

Opal gave Ki a squeeze with both her arms and her legs, cutting off his words. "I don't want to talk anymore, Ki."

They didn't talk anymore.

Chapter 6

The following morning after breakfast Jessie, Ki, and Tess sat together in the common room of the Latrobe ranch house, and Jessie gently questioned the widow about a number of things that were on her mind.

"Tess," she began, "has Arthur Reese or either of the other two men who claim Brent borrowed money from them shown you any documentation of the alleged loans?"

Tess shook her head.

"That strikes me as rather odd," Jessie said.

"Well, it's not odd actually," Tess said. "You see, I questioned Arthur on this very point—it was during his visit here after Brent had been laid out—and he said that he didn't want to trouble me about such matters at such a sad time. Those were his words: 'at such a sad time.' I'm sure he will return here soon to discuss the matter with me as will, no doubt, Addison Chaney and Lon Curlew."

"Instead of waiting for him to come here," Jessie said, "I think it might be a good idea if I had a talk with him at his office in town. Unless, Tess, you would prefer that Ki and I not interfere in such a personal matter."

"Oh, I have not the slightest objection to you talking to Arthur and the others. In fact, I wish you would and the sooner the better. I'll be happy to come with you."

"Why don't you stay here and rest," Jessie suggested. "Ki and I will gather as much information on this matter of Brent's loans as we can and bring it back to you for your consideration."

Tess sat back in her chair with a sigh. "I appreciate the kindness, Jessie, Ki. I truly do. To tell you the truth, I am about worn out. I would sooner go out and plow forty acres as I did when I was young than go through what I have gone through during the past several days."

"We'll be back as soon as we can," Ki told Tess.

Tess rose from her chair a moment after Ki did. She kissed him on the cheek and then turned to Jessie and embraced her. "I don't know what I would do without two good friends such as yourself. I'm so glad you both agreed to stay on here and help me through this terrible time."

"We couldn't do anything else," Jessie said.

"We wouldn't want to do anything else," Ki echoed.

"Bless you both."

An hour later, Jessie left the ranch house and headed for the corral. She was wearing jeans that clung like a second skin to her lithe body, a tan cotton shirt that outlined her full breasts, high-heeled boots, and a black flat-topped Stetson with a chin strap.

When she reached the corral, she hooked a boot on the bottom rail of the enclosure and studied the saddle horses that were milling about inside it. All of them bore the Latrobe Double L brand on their shoulders, and all of them were fine examples of the Latrobe breeding program.

She watched a roan stallion with a blaze, prance and canter a few steps as if showing off for the other confined horses. The horse tossed his coppery mane, snorted several times, and then boldly approached Jessie. She put out a hand. The stallion didn't shy but neither did he touch her hand.

"He likes you," Cass Henderson said as he joined Jessie at the corral. He hooked a boot over the corral's lowest rail, as she had done and added, "Blaze doesn't take to strangers as a rule. But it's clear as well water that he takes to you."

"I'm going into town. Would it be all right if I rode Blaze?"

"I'm certain it would be more than all right, Miss Starbuck. I reckon Blaze would enjoy being ridden by you."

Cass gave her a long look and then returned his attention to the horses in the corral.

His words were harmless enough, Jessie thought, but he had phrased his response to her question in such a way as to make them deliberately ambiguous. He sounded as if he had meant something more than what he had actually said. Something decidedly erotic.

"I'll saddle Blaze for you, Miss Starbuck," Cass offered.

"Thank you. I'd appreciate it. Mr. Henderson—"

He stopped in the act of opening the corral's gate and looked over his shoulder at Jessie.

"Would you also select another horse for Ki and saddle him as well? Ki is coming into town with me."

"Be glad to."

Jessie and Ki rode into El Paso in the early afternoon. They headed down the wide dirt street that was flanked by stores and business offices of all kinds, from pharmacies to attorney's and to land offices. They drew rein and dismounted in front of a two-story clapboard building that bore a gilded legend on the ground floor's large plate glass window: AR-THUR REESE ASSOCIATES.

After wrapping their reins around the hitchrail in front of the building, they went inside.

"We'd like to see Mr. Reese," Ki told the gaunt young man whose neck seemed stretched beyond bearing by the high starched collar he wore.

As if the man had not heard Ki, he continued delicately pecking at the typewriting machine on the desk in front of him.

When Ki repeated his statement, the young man looked up at him and sniffed as if he had smelled something bad. "Mr. Reese is engaged at the moment. Was he expecting you?"

"No, he wasn't," Jessie answered, "but it's important that we talk to him."

"Then you have no appointment. I'm sorry but—"

The young man swiveled around in his chair at the sound of a door opening behind him. A man emerged from the room beyond the door, several envelopes bearing wax seals in his hands.

"Will you see to it that these are dispatched immediately, Wilson," he told the young man before turning on his heels and heading back the way he had come.

"Yes, sir, right away, sir," said the obsequious young man.

"Mr. Reese!" Jessie said sharply, recognizing Arthur Reese, who Tess had pointed out to her at the cemetery. "May we talk to you, please?"

Reese turned and stared at Jessie. "Who, may I ask are you?"

"Miss Jessica Starbuck, Mr. Reese. I'm a friend of Mrs. Latrobe's as is my companion here, Ki."

Something flickered briefly in Reese's eyes. Then he moved toward Jessie and Ki, his hand held out, with a smile on his face that did not reach his eyes. "Miss Starbuck, it's a pleasure to meet you. I've heard of you, of course. You and your father and your various business enterprises." He shook hands with Jessie and then with Ki. "To what do I owe this unexpected visit?"

"May we talk—in there," Jessie asked, indicating the office beyond the open door.

"Yes, of course. Come right in, please do." Reese ushered them into his office, followed them into the room, and closed the door behind him. He showed them to seats in front of his desk and then seated himself behind it.

"We understand from Mrs. Latrobe," Jessie began, "that her husband was deeply in debt to you. Mrs. Latrobe said that you recently informed her of that fact."

"Yes, that is the case. Brent and I did business recently. It seemed he had had some—shall we say, misadventures in his business life of late. He made some serious missteps, as a result he found himself in dire and immediate need of funds. I was happy to lend him the money he needed—on two occasions—and he was, as you might expect, happy to have it."

Ki shifted position in his chair and said, "Mrs. Latrobe, we gather, has no documents supporting these alleged loans, Mr. Reese."

At the word "alleged," Reese's face darkened. But it quickly brightened again. "That is readily understandable under the circumstances, sir."

"What circumstances are those, Mr. Reese?" Ki inquired.

"Brent, as you might imagine, was not very happy about what I referred to a moment ago as his business misadventures. In fact, he was rather sheepish if not shamefaced about them, and he swore me to silence about them. I was not to mention them to Mrs. Latrobe."

"Can you tell us what these 'misadventures' were?" Ki asked.

"I'm sorry. I can't help you there. Brent did not enlighten me on the matter, and I did not pry. It was sufficient for me to know that an old friend needed money and that he was a good risk as we say in the money-lending business. I simply, without further ado, wrote him a draft on the two occasions he came here for help and let the matter go at that."

"Do you know if Mr. Latrobe cashed your drafts, Mr. Reese?" Jessie asked.

"Yes, he did."

"You have, I suppose, the canceled drafts in your possession?" Jessie asked.

"I have. Why do you ask?"

"Forgive me, Mr. Reese," Jessie said, sounding not at all contrite, "but may we see them if it isn't too much trouble?"

"See them? Whatever for, Miss Starbuck?" Reese paused a moment and then said, "I see—I believe I do, yes. You want to verify that the loans to Mr. Brent Latrobe were indeed made as I claim they were."

Jessie said nothing. Neither did Ki.

Reese rose and rounded his desk. He opened the door and stepped out of the office. He could be heard talking in low tones to the young man at the typewriting machine.

Moments later, he returned. In his hand, were two pieces of paper which he handed to Jessie.

She scanned the drafts. One was for sixty thousand dollars and was dated two months earlier; the other was for eighty-five thousand dollars and was dated three months earlier. Both, she noted, had been drawn on Addison Chaney's bank, the El Paso Trust.

She felt a sinking feeling in the pit of her stomach as she stared at the familiar signature that she had seen so many times on letters Brent Latrobe had, in the past, written to both her and her father.

Reese cleared his throat and said, "I had intended to

take these to Tess—to Mrs. Latrobe—and show them to her. After a decent interval had passed, that is."

"Would you allow us to do you that service, Mr. Reese?" Jessie asked sweetly. "We are staying at the Latrobe ranch, and I assure you we would be very careful with these drafts and return them to you just as soon as Tess has had a chance to see them for herself."

"Well," Reese said, hesitating, "if anything should happen to them—"

"If anything should happen to them, Mr. Reese," Ki said evenly, "they would still be recorded in the records of the El Paso Trust, wouldn't they?"

"Why, yes. Yes, they would." Reese turned to Jessie. "You're welcome to take them with you."

"Thank you, sir," Jessie said and got to her feet. She shook hands with Reese and said, "Thank you very much for seeing us when we had no appointment. I know you're a busy man—"

"Never too busy to oblige a friend or, in this case, the lovely representative of my good friend, Mrs. Latrobe."

"One last thing, Mr. Reese," Jessie said. "Did Brent make any payments on those loans before his death?"

"I'm sorry to say he did not."

"Thank you and good day, Mr. Reese."

Ki followed Jessie from the room and out onto the street. "What is it," he asked her. "Is something wrong?"

"Yes, something is wrong. I had hoped—oh, how much I had hoped—that somehow or other this loan business would turn out not to be true. But these drafts"—she held them up—"prove that the loans were made to Brent."

"Maybe we should ask Mrs. Latrobe to verify his signature on the drafts," Ki suggested.

"We will do that, of course. But, as far as I'm concerned, he signed both of these documents. I know Brent's signature. I have ever since I was a girl. It's his all right."

86

"What's our next move?"

"We have to talk to Addison Chaney and to Lon Curlew. I have an idea. To save time, why don't you talk to one of them, and I'll talk to the other. Then we can meet and compare notes back at the ranch later today."

"That's fine with me."

"I'll take Chaney then. You talk to Curlew. See you later at the ranch."

On his way to Elm Street, where Tess had said Lon Curlew's office was located, Ki found himself on Alamo Avenue. He began to notice the houses he was passing, a ramshackle collection of wooden porches and Victorian turrets. One particular house, diagonally across the street, was distinguished by a railroad man's red lantern hanging above its door.

He smiled as he passed the house and turned onto Elm Street, heading for the building directly across the street that bore a sign that said simply: L. CURLEW, ESQUIRE.

Once inside the building, Ki spoke to the matronly woman with the bountiful bosom who was standing behind a long counter.

"I'd like to see Mr. Curlew please."

"I'm sorry. You can't. Mr. Curlew is not in the office at the moment."

"When do you expect him?" Ki asked.

"Mr. Curlew is having a dinner meeting with Mr. Arthur Reese, and he told me not to expect him back before half-past two."

"I wonder if you would be good enough to make an appointment for me with Mr. Curlew for half past two."

"Your name?"

"Ki."

The woman, pencil in hand and bending over a ledger, waited, her pencil poised in mid-air. When Ki said no

87

more, she looked up at him. "Ki what?" she asked with a faint air of exasperation.

"Just Ki."

When she had written his name in the ledger followed by the time, Ki left the office.

As he made his way down the street he glanced at the red light across Alamo Avenue. An idea began to form. Perhaps he could get some information here. He took the steps leading to the porch of the parlor house two at a time. He lifted the heavy brass knocker and rapped it loudly against the door.

A window next to the door was thrown up and a woman's head popped out from between white lace curtains. "We're closed," said the darkly attractive woman of about nineteen or twenty years of age. "Most of the girls are still in bed. Come back after four o'clock."

The woman's head disappeared, but before she could shut the window Ki called out, "Wait!"

Out popped the woman's head again, her face wearing an expression of pique tempered by curiosity. "What do you want?"

"You."

The woman tossed her coal-black curls and gave Ki an impish grin. "Come back after—"

"Please," Ki pleaded with the woman at the window. "I can't come back after four o'clock. I need to talk to you now. You know you're a very lovely lady. I would hate to miss the opportunity to—to—Look, I'll pay you twice your price."

"That would be twenty dollars, you know."

"You're worth twice the price," Ki declared while silently damning himself for his recklessness which, if not quickly curbed, threatened to drive him to the brink of bankruptcy.

The woman shrugged. She gave Ki a wink. "Well, a bird in the hand . . ."

She disappeared from the window in a swirling froth of white lace. A moment later the door opened, and there she was again.

Ki was stunned at his first sight of her. She was willowy with slender limbs. She had small pert breasts like two pillows offering solace to a man's weary head. Her hips curved like a meandering country road. Her wide eyes were as black as her hair. Her full lips were rouged as were her cheeks. Ki guessed at once that she was Mexican even before she said, "My name is Rosa Cortez. Well, don't just stand there. Come on in, big fellow."

Ki took the hand she held out to him and followed her into the parlor that spread out expansively on both sides of the door. It was opulently furnished with heavy claw-footed chairs and a sofa. A brass table sat in the middle of the room. On it sat a lamp with a chimney made of red glass. China spittoons bearing the painted figures of cherubs playing harps, were placed strategically on the floor about the room. From the ceiling hung an enormous crystal chandelier. On one wall was a painting of a buxom woman wearing nothing but a garland of roses in her long fair hair.

Giving him barely enough time to take in the richness of the parlor, Rosa led a reluctant Ki up the stairs to the third floor where she entered a bedroom at the end of a long dark hall. He hung back.

"What's wrong, lover?" Rosa asked.

"I only want answers to a few questions."

"I'll give you answers but let's have some fun first." Her eyes sparked at the handsome man in front of her.

Ki felt his resolve melt. His hands went to the waist of his pants and began to undo his belt.

By the time he had stripped, Rosa was naked and

splashing her body with toilet water from a lime green bottle. Then, she leaned back against a pillow she had plumped up against the bed's headboard.

When he joined her on the bed, she put her arms around him and nipped his ear lobe. He became even harder than he had been, a condition he would have considered impossible a moment ago.

His hands roamed up and down her body, over the mounds of her breasts with their stiffening nipples, down the undulating plain of her belly to the valley between her legs. She wiggled and moaned faintly as the middle finger of his right hand probed her. She was dry but his deft manipulation of her soon set her juices to flowing.

"Before we do it," she murmured, writhing beneath him, "let's take some of this."

"Some of what?" he asked her, slightly annoyed at the distraction that had broken his concentration and momentarily shattered the lustfulness that he had been feeling.

Rosa reached for a bottle that sat on the nightstand beside the bed. Holding it above Ki's back, she reached up with her free hand and uncorked it. Turning her head to the side, she took a swig of the bottle's contents and then offered the bottle to Ki.

He took it from her and sniffed the thick brown liquid the bottle contained.

"Go ahead," Rosa urged. "It makes you feel good. With that stuff, you won't be feeling any pain."

"I don't need laudanum to feel good," Ki said as he put the bottle back on the nightstand.

"I thought all you oriental boys took opium," Rosa said blithely, her eyes beginning to glitter as a result of the dose she had just taken. "I used to work in a house up north near where the Union Pacific was being built, and we used to get a lot of Celestials as trade. They all used opium."

"I'm not a Celestial," Ki said, using the word by which many referred to Chinese people.

"You're not?"

"I'm Japanese. That is, my mother was. My father was an American. Now, what do you say we get on with the business at hand, honey?"

"Why, sure thing." Rosa reached out, took another swig from the bottle of laudanum, and then put it back. "Now then," she said in a surprisingly sober voice. "Are you going to do it to me the Japanese or the American way?"

Three minutes later, Rosa, greatly aroused as Ki thrust rhythmically within her, cried out. "I don't know which way this is that you're doing it, but don't stop. Don't you *dare* stop!"

Ki didn't.

He plowed. He plunged. He bucked and bounced upon the lush body beneath him. He felt as if the top of his head was about to blow away. He felt as if forces far beyond his control were gathering in his body and centering in his loins where an explosion of world-shaking proportions was about to take place.

He seemed to soar as he came. Rosa's fingernails tore at his back and her hot lips nibbled his neck.

She came a moment after he did. She was breathing even harder than Ki was. Her eyes were closed, her lips parted, her warm breath gusted past Ki's ear.

Ki's body continued to slap sweatily against Rosa's. Then, finally, he lay quiet but still panting upon her, and she, cooing like a dove in a dovecote, threw out her arms and lay thoroughly relaxed on the bed.

"I'm a working girl, as you know," she murmured, "but this isn't work. This is pure pleasure. If I'd known it was going to be that good, I wouldn't have bothered taking that dope."

"Thanks."

91

"Are you from El Paso?"

"Nope."

"Where are you from?"

"The northwestern part of the state."

"You married?"

Ki shook his head and withdrew from Rosa. As he flopped down on his back on the bed, she turned on her side, propped her head up on one hand, and stared down at him.

"What are you doing in El Paso?"

"You sure are about as curious as any cat I ever met."

"I like you. I want to know things about you. You never even told me your name."

"It's Ki. Now it's time for me to ask some questions. Did you know Brent Latrobe?"

Rosa fell back on the bed. "That sure was a shame about Mr. Latrobe killing himself like he did. I used to run into him on the street. He never came here or anyplace like this. He was too much in love with his wife. He was always nice and polite to me. He didn't treat me or any of the other girls like whores. He treated us like we were just as good as anybody."

"In my opinion, you are, and he was right to do what you say he did." Ki's right index finger touched the curved tip of Rosa's nose.

"A lot of people were jealous of Mr. Latrobe."

Ki wiggled his finger, gently squashing the tip of Rosa's nose. "They were? Why?"

"Because he was rich. You know, successful and all."

"Who was jealous of him?"

"Oh, I don't know. A lot of people. People like Mr. Chaney at the bank. Him and Mr. Curlew—he's a big-shot cattleman. But they didn't mean a hill of beans to Mr. Latrobe from what I hear. He wasn't the least bit scared of any of them, Mr. Arthur hoity-toity Reese included."

Ki withdrew his finger from Rosa's nose. "It's funny you should mention those names. I happened to pay a visit with a friend of mine to Mr. Reese before I came here. And I'm going to meet with Mr. Lon Curlew at half-past two this afternoon."

"Some people don't care what kind of company they keep, I guess."

Ki, intrigued by what Rosa had been saying, asked, "What's that supposed to mean?"

"Nothing."

"Come on, honey, tell me." He bent and licked the nipple on her left breast, causing a tremor to travel through Rosa's body.

"People say, some do, that those men won't stop at anything to get what they want. I happen to know for a fact that what some people say happens to be true in at least one case that I know about personally."

"Tell me about it."

The glitter put in Rosa's eyes by the opium in the laudanum she had taken earlier gave way to a warm glow. "There's this man who comes here. He always asks for me."

"I can understand why."

Rosa, beaming, raised her head and kissed Ki's cheek. "His name's Roark. Tough as hickory and he has about as much sense as hickory has too. He told me once how he and some other Texas trash were hired by Arthur Reese to run-off some settlers that were squatting on land he coveted. The sodbusters all had title to their lands, but that didn't make no never-mind to Reese. Roark said he and the other rowdies Reese hired ran those settlers as far east as Louisiana, and not one of them has ever come back here. Reese bought their land when they defaulted on their mortgage payments, and it was Addison Chaney over at the El Paso Trust who put their land up for auction."

Ki's mind was racing. Was Rosa telling the truth? Had the man named Roark told her the truth or had he been merely bragging about him being a bad man?

"You going to be in town long?" Rosa asked.

Ki, brought abruptly back from his speculations, said, "I don't know how long exactly."

"You'll come see me again if you can?"

"I will. That's a promise." Ki sealed it with a kiss.

When he was dressed and ready to leave, he paid Rosa the forty dollars he had promised her.

"It's none of my business, Ki, but do you mind if I give you some advice?"

"Not at all."

"You'll do well to be on your toes where Lon Curlew and his friends are concerned. If you cross them you could be in big trouble. More trouble maybe than you can handle."

Chapter 7

Jessie had taken an almost instant dislike to Addison Chaney from the moment she entered his office. There was something about the man, something she could not quite put her finger on, that set her teeth on edge.

Now, as he blustered and stalked about his office like a wild boar, she found herself disliking him even more.

"I don't see that this matter is any of your business, Miss Starbuck," Chaney bellowed, his hands folded behind his back as he paced, his head bent as if to see the carpeted path before him. "You are not a blood relative of the deceased nor are you authorized in any formal legal way, by your own admission, to inquire into the matter."

"Mr. Chaney," Jessie said, her hands gripping the arms of the chair in which she was seated as she forced herself to remain calm despite her growing impatience with this florid-faced fat man, "I merely asked you to confirm that Brent Latrobe had indeed placed himself in your debt."

Chaney stopped pacing and spun around, his chins waggling, to stare with cold eyes at Jessie. "I have done that very thing, Miss Starbuck."

"No, sir, you have not. Oh, yes, you have stated that you had granted Mr. Latrobe a mortgage on his homestead. But I asked—and I admit I may not have made myself clear on this point—to see some documentation of that alleged fact."

"Miss Starbuck," Chaney said in a frozen voice, "I am, as I have repeatedly pointed out to you here today, under no obligation to provide you with so much as the time of day, never mind documentation of this bank's business dealings with its clients."

"Do I understand you to say, Mr. Chaney, that you refuse to show me proof that the mortgage you claim to hold actually exists?"

Chaney strode to his desk and slammed a fist down upon it. "Miss Starbuck, I know you are a woman of wealth and power in this state, indeed in the nation at large. But let me make one thing very clear to you. I am not and will not be intimidated by your posturing and blatant interference in what was a private matter between me and Brent Latrobe and is now a private matter between the widow of the late lamented and myself. When Mrs. Latrobe sees fit to call on me here at my office, I shall show her the document in question.

"Now I have nothing more to say to you, Miss Starbuck. Except for this. I must ask you to leave my office. I am a busy man."

"Mr. Chaney, did you know that Mrs. Latrobe believes that her husband did not commit suicide?"

Chaney went behind his desk and threw himself into an upholstered chair that groaned beneath his weight. "I have heard gossip to that effect, yes. I believe Mrs. Latrobe has spoken of her belief to numerous people." Chaney *tsk-tsked*. "Poor Mrs. Latrobe is obviously quite undone by her grief."

"I take it you do believe Brent Latrobe hanged himself."

"I most certainly do. Marshal Hayes found the man hanging in his office. The coroner gave a broken neck as the cause of death. Surely, you do not expect me to believe the wild words and wilder speculations of a woman who is apparently unable to face what I admit is a most unpleasant truth. Namely, that her husband died by his own hand."

"As I told you, Mr. Chaney, when I first arrived here in your office, Mrs. Latrobe has asked me and my friend, Ki, to look into the circumstances of her husband's passing. That is why I came here to talk to you. I regret your lack of cooperation, Mr. Chaney. But Ki and I will continue looking into this matter, with or without your cooperation."

"You call it 'looking into this matter,'" Chaney snarled as Jessie rose and started for the door. Without leaving his seat, a subtle insult to Jessie, he added, "I call it meddling, and meddling, young woman, can get a meddler in a great deal of trouble."

Jessie, her anger finally boiling over, turned sharply so that she was again facing Chaney. "Is that a threat?"

He threw up his hands in a mock gesture of surprise. "A threat? Why, no, not at all, Miss Starbuck. Call it a word to the wise."

As Jessie opened the office door, Chaney added, "You do know the expression, Miss Starbuck? 'A word to the wise is sufficient?' I hope my word to you will be sufficient so that we may avoid any possible future unpleasantness."

"I intend to tell you absolutely nothing about my dealings with Brent Latrobe, young man," said Lon Curlew as he sat in the large chair behind his desk in his neat office, his cane resting on the top of his desk. "I want to make that clear to you from the outset. I am a man who does not mince words. Now you know where I stand in this matter. Just as I told Arthur—"

"Arthur Reese, you mean?" Ki interrupted.

"Arthur was telling me at our dinner meeting today about the visit you and your ladyfriend paid him earlier today."

Ki thought Curlew had made the word 'ladyfriend' sound obscene.

"Arthur said that he had shown you the drafts of the two loans he made to Brent Latrobe. He also told me that, in his opinion, there was a very good chance that you or your ladyfriend or both of you would be coming to talk to me about the chattel mortgage I hold on the Double L stock."

"And here I am," Ki said in a tone he perversely hoped Curlew would find taunting. He wanted to provoke the man. More than once he had found that a man provoked is a man likely to make mistakes. In this case, he hoped, a provoked Curlew might provide him, unwittingly perhaps, with information about Brent Latrobe and his business dealings that just might shed some light on the manner of the man's death.

But Curlew calmed down. His bald head, was, however, coated with a thin sheen of sweat, which did not escape Ki's notice.

"You march in here," Curlew continued, "as if you expected me to just sit down and open my books to you."

"I hoped you would, Mr. Curlew. I still hope you will."

"Well, I won't!"

"What do you have to hide, Mr. Curlew?"

Ki thought the stockman was about to explode. His eyes bugged out. His face grew flushed. His teeth ground together and a muscle in his jaw jumped.

"Would whatever it is you're hiding," Kit said glibly, "have anything to do with Mr. Latrobe's death?"

This time Curlew did explode. He bellowed like a bull caught in a canebreak. His lips flapped together and saliva flew from between them.

"Why, you impertinent little pup!" he finally managed to roar. "How dare you suggest that I have anything to hide? I am a respectable businessman. My dealings have always been above suspicion. My life is an open book—"

"But your stock company's books aren't open."

"No, they are not. Not to you or to any other Tom, Dick, or Harry who happens to come waltzing in here suggesting that there is something wrong with the way I do business."

"Why don't you put me in my place, Curlew? Show me the legal instrument that substantiates your claim on the Latrobe stock."

"I'll show you nothing. I'll—"

There was a soft knock on the office door.

"Go away!" shouted an exasperated Curlew.

The door opened.

Ki turned to find Marshal Buck Hayes standing, hat in hand, in the open doorway.

"What do you want, Hayes?" Curlew asked, impatiently drumming the fingers of his right hand on his desk.

"I just ran into Mr. Reese, Mr. Curlew," Hayes replied. "He told me you and him had just finished having dinner over at Mrs. Malone's boarding house. He also told me about being pestered by this fellow here and Miss Starbuck. He said you might be the next one to be pestered and maybe I ought to call on you to see if—"

"I am indeed being pestered, Marshal," Curlew interrupted, an evil grin forming on his face. "By this impertinent young man you see here before you. It was good of Arthur to alert you to that unwelcome possibility. Now it remains only for you to do your duty where this interloper is concerned."

"I take it he's trespassing."

"He is. What's more, he is disturbing the peace—my peace."

99

"Well, El Paso has laws against both of those crimes in case folk take a notion, like this jasper has, to commit them."

"This is a public business office," Ki pointed out. "I cannot be trespassing in a *public* place. As for disturbing the peace, if there's been any disturbance of anybody's peace, it's the result of Mr. Curlew shouting at the top of his voice instead of carrying on his side of our conversation in a gentlemanly tone."

"Arrest him, Marshal!" Curlew roared, pointing his cane at Ki.

"Come along, you," Hayes said to Ki.

When Ki didn't move, Hayes drew his revolver. "You fixing to move, mister, or do I have to move you?"

Ki hesitated. Then, shrugging, he left the office, followed by Buck Hayes whose gun remained in his hand.

"That way," Hayes ordered, gesturing with his gun as he emerged from the office behind Ki.

Ki walked in the direction Hayes had indicated, aware of Curlew standing in the window of his office, a look of triumph on his face.

Five minutes later, he was inside the Marshal's office. Two minutes after that, he was locked in a cell in the marshal's jail.

When Jessie returned to the Latrobe ranch, she found that Tess was not there. Upon questioning the housekeeper, she learned that Tess had driven into El Paso. Yes, the journey had been unexpected. The missus, said the housekeeper, decided to make the trip on the spur of the moment. No, she didn't know what the reason for the trip was. The missus said she would return by late afternoon.

Jessie went to the window of the common room and looked up. The sun was already halfway down to the western horizon so Tess should be returning soon.

She was about to move away from the window when she heard a loud sound, a sound she recognized at once as the sound of wood shattering. She hurried outside and around the house in search of the source of the sound. She quickly found it. One of the top rails of the corral had been split in two. She saw at once what had done the splitting.

The huge stallion was rearing up on his hind legs; his front legs pawed the air wildly. Cass Henderson tightly gripped the end of the lariat that he had placed around the horse's neck and darted from side to side in an effort to stay out of the way of the stallion's flailing front hooves. The horse Cass was trying to control danced this way and that on his strong hind legs.

Jessie stopped and watched the battle that was raging between man and beast.

Cass, as the horse's hooves slammed down upon the ground like two iron anvils, deftly wrapped the end of the lariat around a snubbing post in the center of the corral. Then, moving up along the taut rope with a bridle in his hand, he warily approached the horse. Though the animal tried to toss his head, Cass soon had the bridle in place.

Picking up a blanket from the ground, Cass draped it over the horse's head. Blinded, the animal stood his ground, almost motionless. Cass took down a saddle that rested on one of the corral rails. Hooking its stirrups onto the saddle horn to keep them out of the way, he placed the saddle on the stallion's back.

The horse tried to buck as Cass, hunkering down, tightened the cinch strap under the animal's barrel. Then Cass flipped down the stirrups, stepped gracefully into the saddle, removed the blanket, and then the lariat that was around the horse's neck. Cass gripped the reins in his right hand, the saddle horn in his left.

The horse sunfished, his four legs coming together beneath his sharply arched body as it left the ground.

101

Cass stayed in the saddle but lost his hat.

As the horse spun in a circle, Cass caught sight of Jessie watching him. He gave her a mile-wide grin, and she, impressed by his daring that was accompanied by a kind of incredible nonchalance as evidenced by his grin and his having let go of the saddle horn to wave to her, waved and smiled back at him.

When Cass weathered a particularly vicious attempt on the part of the horse to dislodge him, Jessie enthusiastically applauded his efforts to break the stallion.

Then she gasped as the horse suddenly leaped into the air and twisted violently to one side.

Cass was thrown out of the saddle and Jessie winced at the loud thud his body made as it hit the hardpacked earth.

"Look out!" she cried as the stallion made for the man.

Cass nimbly scrambled out of the path of the charging horse. He scooped up the blanket he had used earlier to blind the horse so that he could put the bridle in place. Then he lunged at the animal getting a foot in a stirrup as he did so. An instant later, he was back in the saddle. This time when the horse bucked, he hazed it with the blanket, hitting the stallion on the flanks, on the head, the face, the withers. The unrelenting punishment cowed the stallion in less than five minutes, allowing Cass to ride him to a standstill.

Cass sat his saddle for another minute or two to show the horse who was the winner of their battle. Then he slid out of the saddle. Dropping the blanket, he stripped the gear from the horse he had broken and made his way over to where Jessie still stood watching him with admiration in her eyes.

"Afternoon," he said, his chest heaving as he tried to catch his breath.

"That was a fine job you just did," Jessie told him.

"It's one I almost didn't get to do," Cass said a bit

sheepishly, glancing at the blown horse that stood feebly pawing the dirt while strings of saliva dripped from his lips and sweat shone on his body. "That critter knows more tricks than old Satan himself and what's more he can move as fast as a turpentined cat."

Jessie smiled.

"If you'll excuse me, Miss Starbuck, I'll take him into the barn and wipe him down, give him a good long drink of water."

Without waiting for a response from Jessie, he went back and refastened the lariat around the horse's neck.

Jessie watched Cass lead the stallion from the corral and head for the barn. She expected him to look back at her. When he didn't, she decided the next move was up to her. She went into the corral, picked up Cass's hat which he had evidently forgotten, and followed him into the dim barn that smelled of old leather, straw, and dried horse droppings.

She stood beside the stall in which Cass had placed the horse and watched as the ranch foreman, with his back to her, firmly but gently wiped the animal down with a clean cotton cloth. She listened as he spoke to the horse he had just conquered.

"Cooo—eee, but you sure did put up a fight," Cass said as he worked on the horse. "You got yourself a heart as big as a barn and every inch of it's a fighter's heart. You got nothing to be ashamed of. You put up a fight to be proud of. You were pure hell on the hoof."

Cass ducked under the stallion's head and as he came up on the animal's other side he was facing Jessie.

"Hey," he exclaimed. "I didn't know you were there. If I had, I wouldn't have cursed like I just did."

"You forgot your hat," Jessie said and handed it to him.

He reached out for it and then clapped it on his head. "My ma, she used to say I had such a bad memory I'd

103

forget my head were it not fastened to my neck."

When Jessie said nothing, Cass asked, "Did you find out anything in town today?"

"I found out that Mr. Latrobe did accept two drafts from Arthur Reese, both of them for substantial amounts of money."

"Then Mrs. Latrobe, she was wrong about the old man not being deep in debt when he died."

"Yes, it appears that she was, I'm sorry to say."

Cass continued grooming the stallion in a thoughtful silence that Jessie shared with him.

She watched his strong hands move and before long it seemed to her that she could feel them touching *her* body, gliding sensuously over *her* skin. . . .

When he looked up at her again, she said, "You're good with horses."

"I've had me some pretty good teachers in my time. Mr. Latrobe, he was one of them. Then too there was my pa. He was always an easy man with all kinds of critters: horses, dogs, even wild animals. He could, my ma swore, charm a squirrel right out of the tree and a skunk out of its hideyhole. Which was a darn good thing, my ma said, on account of we were as poor as church mice, and pa didn't always have cash nor credit neither to buy shells for his hunting rifle. I guess I take after him where knowing how to treat live things so they don't go skittish on me is concerned."

Jessie watched the stallion's skin ripple as he shuddered with pleasure at Cass' touch. She found herself identifying with the horse, found herself envying the animal, found herself wanting to be touched by the ranch foreman's strong but gentle hands.

"If I had the same touch where women are concerned," Cass said with a glance in Jessie's direction, "I wouldn't still be single."

104

"Maybe what you need is some practice," Jessie suggested.

"You know something," he said, stopping work and resting his forearms on the horse's back, the cotton cloth that was now wet with the animal's sweat held loosely in his right hand. "You might be right about that."

Their eyes met, held.

Cass dropped the cloth. He left the stall and came around to where Jessie was standing. She turned to face him. He rested his hands lightly on her shoulders and then drew her toward him.

Jessie closed her eyes as his lips met hers.

A moment later, her heart pounding, she said, "I was wrong."

"About what?" he asked as he held her tightly, the warmth of her body inflaming his own.

"You don't need practice with women. You've obviously had a great deal of it."

This time Jessie was the aggressor. She drew Cass' head toward her and kissed him again. When his tongue invaded her mouth she met it with her own.

"Up there," he said a moment later, drawing away from her and pointing to the ladder that led to the hay loft. "Nobody will bother us up there."

Jessie proceeded him up the ladder and lay down in the dry and sweet-smelling hay that filled the loft. Cass joined her and they locked together in a passionate embrace.

Jessie finally broke their embrace. She unbuttoned her jeans and pulled them down. She practically tore her shirt from her body. She watched Cass do the same. Then she held up her arms to him and he sank down upon her with a sigh and an exhalation of breath that was hot upon her cheek.

He adroitly adjusted his body to cover hers. He nudged her legs farther apart with his own. Then he was fingering

105

her but he quickly found out that such ministrations were unnecessary. She was not merely moist; her juices drowned his probing finger.

Fully aroused now, his staff throbbed and spasmed as it poled its way into her. He raised his upper body, supporting himself on his hands, so that he could look down at Jessie as he began to move with tantalizing slowness within her.

He watched her eyes take on that glow that desire always kindles in passionate women. He stoked that fire with his iron-hard shaft that was buried deep inside the woman under him who twisted from side to side while simultaneously thrusting her pelvis up to draw him even more deeply into her body as she sought his satisfaction along with her own.

"Is it—" he began.

"It's good," she whispered between clenched teeth as her hands rose and clasped his shoulders. "Oh, it's so good. So *wonderful*."

She groaned as he inadvertently, in his enthusiastic thrusting, slipped out of her. She seized his shaft and blindly, almost instinctively, placed it within her again. Her body closed upon it, massaged it.

Cass threw back his head; his eyes closed now, his lips parted. He could feel the mounting tension that preceded the thrilling climax that he knew was coming, was now only moments away. He shifted position slightly—drawing out the pleasure that was a kind of exquisite agony. Then he came. His body shuddered. He cried out, a kind of animalistic howl. He dropped back down upon Jessie. His hands went under her buttocks. He lifted her up toward him and held her there as he continued to shoot a steady stream of his seed into her.

Jessie cried out and bit down on her lower lip as she too came.

Cass drew a deep breath and buried his face in her neck,

becoming aware of the sweet clean smell of her copper-blond hair. He raised his head slightly and kissed her ear, her chin, her nose, her lips.

She eased down on the hay until she was able to touch his nipples with her hot lips. She went from one to the other and back again, tasting, biting, teasing.

Cass responded. He held Jessie close, mindful of her fingernails raking his back and buttocks, the slight pain adding spice to their second coupling.

This time Jessie came first but she continued to match Cass's wild rhythm until he too exploded.

Only then did she release her hold on him. Only then did a drained but satisfied Cass withdraw from her and flop down by her side.

Jessie took his right hand in hers. She kissed it, turned it over, tongued his palm.

With his free left hand, Cass fondled her breasts, tweaking her erect nipples between his fingers. Jessie dropped his hand and gripped his still-stiff shaft. She stroked it lightly at first, then more strenuously.

Cass was about to tell her it was no use, that he was empty. Jessie proved him wrong. Not once but twice over the next uncounted number of delightful minutes.

As Jessie and Cass left the barn, Tess drove up to the front door of the ranch house in a black fringe-topped surrey.

"Cass, I've got to talk to her," Jessie said, using the ranch foreman's first name as she had begun to do in the last few minutes in the barn just as he had stopped calling her Miss Starbuck. "I'll see you later."

"I'll go along with you, Jessie," he said. "I have something to turn over to Mrs. Latrobe. I went to the house to hand it over before I went to work on that stallion, but she'd gone into town."

107

The pair made their way toward the surrey in which a pensive Tess still sat as if lost in thought.

As they drew near it, Tess noticed them. She waved a greeting to them.

Jessie and Cass reached the surrey just as Tess stepped down from it.

"Mrs. Latrobe, I've got something to give you," Cass said. He dug down into a pocket of his jeans and came up with a small blue box stamped Tiffany & Co., New York City, and a long white envelope which he handed to Tess. "I thought I'd best wait," he said, "till things had settled down some—I mean till the funeral was over and all—before I gave you these."

Tess took the box and the envelope from him and asked, "What are these, Cass?"

"They're the presents Mr. Latrobe got you for your wedding anniversary. He asked me to hold on to them. He said if he hid them anywheres in the house you'd be sure to find them and spoil his surprise."

Tess smiled and then opened the box Cass had given her.

Jessie leaned forward so that she could see what the box contained. "Oh, Tess, it's lovely!"

Tess stared down at the jeweled brooch in the shape of a tiger that the box contained. The tiger's eyes were rubies; its stripes diamonds. Tess clasped it to her breast.

"What's in the envelope, Tess?" Jessie asked.

She proceeded to open it. She unfolded the piece of paper the envelope contained, read it, and then handed it to Jessie who examined what turned out to be a telegraph message addressed to Brent Latrobe from the Pyramid Hotel in Austin, Texas confirming his request for a double room for a week. Written on the message were the words:

"We'll have a second honeymoon, Tess, at long last."

• • •

Recognizing the handwriting as Brent Latrobe's, Jessie was reminded of the two drafts she had in her pocket, the ones given her by Arthur Reese.

"These gifts prove that Brent did not commit suicide," Tess said. "Why would he bother to buy me this brooch and make these reservations if he planned to kill himself?"

"Tess—" Jessie began, but was interrupted.

"I was right to do what I just did," Tess said firmly as if she were talking to herself. "This proves that I was right in doing what I did."

Cass glanced at Jessie who then asked, "What did you do, Tess?"

"After you and Ki left earlier today, I kept going over things in my mind. I found I just couldn't sit still and do nothing. I decided to go to El Paso and send a telegraph message to the governor.

"Brent and I and Bill Kirkland were good friends long before Bill was elected governor. I decided Bill was someone who could help me. I asked him to appoint a special prosecutor to look into the matter of Brent's death.

"What I did is no reflection on you or Ki, Jessie. I know you both will do all you can to help me. But I thought a special prosecutor might be able to do even more. You do understand?"

"Of course, I do," Jessie said.

"Did you and Ki find out anything in town?" Tess asked, a note of hopefulness in her voice.

"We talked to Arthur Reese."

"What did Arthur have to say?"

"He confirmed that Brent had borrowed from him on two occasions as you told us earlier."

Jessie withdrew from her pocket the two drafts Reese had given her. She handed them to Tess who took them and examined them closely, her face paling as she did so.

"That's Brent's signature on those drafts, isn't it?" Jessie asked.

Tess's lips moved but no words were audible.

"What did you say, Tess?" Jessie asked.

"I said yes, that's Brent's handwriting on these drafts."

"Forgive me for saying this, Tess, but Brent's debts might have overwhelmed him and caused him to—to take his own life."

"Did you find similar documents when you talked to Addison Chaney and Lon Curlew?"

"Mr. Chaney refused to show me the mortgage he claims to hold on the homestead," Jessie answered. "Ki was to have talked to Mr. Curlew. But he hasn't returned from town yet so I don't know what, if anything, he found out."

Tess looked down at the two drafts she held in her right hand. Then her gaze shifted to her left hand which held the box containing the brooch from Tiffany's and the telegraph message from the Pyramid Hotel in Austin.

She looked up at Jessie and Cass, her face still pale. "I don't understand," she said. "I simply do not understand any of this," she repeated in the plaintive voice of a child who has been punished for reasons she cannot comprehend.

Chapter 8

Ki sat on the bunk in the dank jail cell where Marshal Buck Hayes had placed him. His back was braced against the wooden wall, and his legs were folded under him. His hands rested in his lap.

The steady *drip-drip-a-drip-drip* from a leaky pump handle beyond the wall drifted through the barred window, and somewhere in the distance a dog barked as if it would never stop. Otherwise, all was quiet in the jail.

Through the open door that led to the office in the front of the building, Ki could see Hayes seated at his battered desk. The marshal's booted feet were propped up on the desk, his large hands folded comfortably over his belly, and his hat pulled down over his eyes as he dozed.

The front door of the marshal's office suddenly flew open and banged back against the wall, startling Hayes who swung his feet down from his desk and pushed his hat back on his head as he sat up in his chair.

"Oh, it's you, darlin'," Hayes said to his daughter as Opal rushed across the room to plant a kiss on her father's forehead. "How are you today?"

"I'm fine, Papa. Well, no I'm not actually."

"What's troubling my best girl?"

"It's that Mr. Reese."

"Why, what's Arthur Reese done to upset you?"

Ki watched a pout form on Opal's pretty face which, he thought, made her look even prettier than usual.

"He sent me some more flowers. Black-eyed Susans this time."

"In my day a girl would be pleased to receive flowers from a gentleman. Especially from a gentleman of stature and means such as Arthur Reese."

"Well, *I'm* not pleased," Opal declared. "I wish he would keep his flowers—and himself—to himself."

Hayes pulled Opal down so that she was half-sitting on the arm of his chair. "Playing hard to get, are you?"

"Papa, what an awful thing to say!"

Hayes chucked his daughter teasingly under the chin. "It won't be long before all the men and boys in El Paso will be lining up at our front door. They will be just as soon as word gets to all of them that you're home, as it has apparently gotten to Arthur Reese."

"Well, I hope Mr. Reese isn't anywhere on the line when and if it forms. That man makes me feel creepy, Papa. It's the way he looks at me. I declare, when he looks at me I feel as if I don't have a single stitch of clothes on. It's embarrassing."

"If you feel that way, darlin', why don't you just tell him that you're busy? Tell him your dance card is all filled up, thank you just the same."

"I have told him," Opal insisted. "Repeatedly. He won't take no for an answer. He even said something about having a talk with you if I didn't begin to show some interest in him. Can you imagine? Does he think you have some secret way of making me pay attention to a man I can't abide?"

Hayes suddenly shot to his feet, dislodging Opal from her precarious perch on the arm of his chair.

Ki heard him mutter something that was not clear which was followed by Opal's perfectly clear exclamation, "Papa, don't curse and carry on so! If I thought the matter of Mr. Reese paying unwelcome attention to me would upset you, I'd have said not a word about it to you."

Opal crossed the room and sat down in a chair next to a rifle rack. As she did so, she caught sight of Ki in the cell beyond the door. She let out a little cry of surprise and sprang to her feet.

Ki nodded to her but said nothing.

"Papa," Opal cried, turning on her father while pointing in the opposite direction at Ki, "what is *he* doing in there?"

"It seems we can't avoid the subject of Arthur Reese," a still somewhat testy Hayes told his daughter.

"What does that mean?"

"Reese told me earlier today that Ki and his friend, Miss Starbuck, had been in his office asking all kinds of questions about Brent Latrobe's business dealing with him. He told me he wouldn't be surprised if that pair of outsiders wouldn't try to make trouble for others in town as well. He told me to look in on Addison Chaney and Lon Curlew to see if they were having any similar problems. Sure enough, I found Ki in Curlew's office and Curlew in a rage over the man's impertinent questioning about Curlew's relationship with Brent Latrobe."

"You locked Ki up because he was asking Mr. Curlew questions?" a clearly incredulous Opal asked.

"Curlew is a power in this town, Opal. Don't you lose sight of that important fact. The man said Ki was trespassing and disturbing the peace. He wanted Ki arrested."

"So you arrested him."

"I did."

"Papa, Ki is a friend of mine."

113

"I don't care whether he is or not, Opal. The man broke the law and he has to pay for it."

"Papa, let him go."

"Darlin', you know I can't do that. He has to appear before Judge Davis to answer the charges Curlew has brought against him."

Opal, her fists clenched at her sides, turned on her heels and hurried to the door of Ki's cell.

Ki got up from his bunk to meet her, the cell's bars an iron barrier separating them. "Hello, Opal."

"Ki, this is awful—you being in there, I mean. I can't imagine what ever possessed my father to lock you up like this. I'm sure you're no criminal."

Ki reached through the bars and gently touched Opal's cheek with the tips of his fingers. "You should always wear pink," he said. "It become you."

Opal looked down at her pink dress with the red panels in the skirt and the clutch of paper roses pinned to its bodice. "I've had this old thing for years."

"Thanks for trying to get me out of here. It's obvious that your father is too stubborn to listen to reason."

Opal's expression darkened. "My father is not stubborn, I'll have you know. He is a man of honor. One who does his duty. A man who—"

Ki held up a hand and took a step backward into the cell. "I'll say no more."

"You had just better not say another word against my father. He has a job to do and he does it fearlessly, protecting the rich as well as the poor."

"I don't know how good he is at protecting the poor," Ki couldn't keep himself from saying with a faint trace of bitterness, "but he sure does a fine enough job protecting rich men like Lon Curlew from dangerous criminals like myself. At the behest, I might add, of another rich man. Namely, your would-be suitor, Arthur Reese."

114

"You heard? You were eavesdropping all the time and you heard every word I said to papa!"

"Opal, honey, I couldn't help hearing. The door was open and the two of you were not exactly whispering."

"I didn't know anyone was here."

Ki shrugged, spreading his hands out in a gesture that might have been apologetic.

Opal bit her lower lip. She tried to look indignant but succeeded only in looking amused despite the angry words she had just hurled at Ki.

Finally, she stepped closer to the bars and beckoned to Ki. When he took up his former position on the other side of the bars, she whispered, "I should tell Mr. Reese that you and I are—good friends. Maybe that would discourage him."

"If I were out of this cage, I would discourage him— and I don't mean with words."

"Oh, Ki, what a gentlemanly thing to say. I didn't know you would be my knight in shining armor."

"I'd like to be. But I can't be—not while I'm cooped up in here."

"I'll talk to father again. Surely, I can make him listen to reason—make him release you. In my custody, perhaps."

"I would like that," Ki said sincerely. "But I don't think you'll have much luck with him. There is one way though that might get me out of here."

"What is it?"

"If you would ride out to the Latrobe ranch and tell Jessie where I am, she might be able to talk some sense into your papa."

"I'll go tell her. I'll go right now."

"I'll be forever in your debt, Opal."

"Careful, Ki," Opal said, wiggling a playful finger

through the bars at him. "I am very good at collecting on debts owed to me."

Ki watched her go flouncing through the door, past her father without a word, and on out of the office.

"Of course, papa was just doing his job," Opal said to Jessie as they rode into El Paso together. "But I wish he wouldn't let Mr. Curlew and men like him tell him what to do, as was the case with Ki."

"Rich men like Curlew," Jessie said, "have power. They can often dictate the way city government is run by trying to control the men who make up that government."

"Papa was always such an independent sort of man," Opal mused. "But since I've been back I've noticed a change in him. He seems—I don't quite know how to put this—fidgety. Afraid of his own shadow. It's so unlike him."

The women drew rein in front of the marshal's office and dismounted. After wrapping their reins around the hitchrail in front of the building, they went inside.

Marshal Hayes, at his desk, looked up as the women entered and frowned.

"Marshal," Jessie said, not bothering with any pleasantries, "I've come to post bail for Ki."

"Have you now?" Hayes gave Opal a withering glare. "You brought this woman here?" he asked her.

"Yes, Papa. She's a friend of Ki's—as I am."

"Why must you meddle, Opal, in things that don't concern you?"

"But Papa this thing does concern me. I told you Ki is my friend."

"You'll get us both in trouble, Opal," Hayes said, "if you can't or won't learn to let sleeping dogs lie."

"Papa, I don't understand. What—"

"Go home, Opal," Hayes ordered. "Now."

116

Opal started to protest but a peremptory gesture from her father stopped her. She left without another word.

"How much, Marshal?"

"What are you talking about, Miss Starbuck?"

"You know very well what I'm talking about, Marshal. I'm talking about bail for Ki. How much is it?"

"Ki stays right where he is until he can stand trial."

Jessie folded her arms. She silently warned herself not to lose her temper with this obdurate man. "If necessary, Marshal, I will hire the best lawyer in El Paso to arrange for Ki's bail. I will also ask that same lawyer to investigate your qualifications to hold this office. When he makes known to the general public that you have denied bail to a prisoner who is being held merely on misdemeanor charges, not felony charges, I think your conduct in office may very well be called into question. That may, in turn, lead to your removal from office for just cause."

Hayes smiled. He tried a little laugh. "So the high and mighty Miss Starbuck is threatening me, is she?"

"Threatening you, Marshal? Not at all. I am merely outlining for you the course of action I plan to take if you insist upon remaining uncooperative. I had hoped and continue to hope that we can settle this unpleasant matter amicably and according to law."

"Go ahead. Hire yourself a lawyer. Ki stays right where he is."

"I take it, then, that you are confident your record in office, your qualifications for the job, your background and character, Marshal, are all above reproach and can stand prosecutorial investigation."

"Meddlers!" Hayes snarled, jumping up from behind his desk. "First my daughter, now you. It's enough to drive a good man to deviltry. I swear it is. All right, Miss Starbuck. I don't want any trouble. Your friend in the cell back

117

there isn't worth it and neither are you. One hundred dollars."

Jessie's expression didn't change but, when she spoke, her voice was cold. "One hundred dollars, Marshal? Isn't that a rather exorbitant amount of bail necessary to obtain the release of a person accused of committing just two misdemeanors?"

"If you can't pay it, your friend stays in jail."

"Oh, I can pay it," Jessie said, counting out one hundred dollars from the roll of paper money she had taken from the pocket of her jeans. "Did you think—or hope—I couldn't? Is that why you set such an inappropriately high bail, Marshal?"

Instead of answering Jessie, Hayes picked up a ring of keys from his desk and went through the door leading to the jail cells. When he returned, Ki was with him.

"It's good to see you, Jessie," Ki said.

"Are you all right?"

"I'm fine. But hungry. Marshal Hayes doesn't hang his criminals. It appears to me that he starves them to death."

"Come on," Jessie said. "We'll get something to eat."

As they were leaving the office, Hayes called out to them, "If either one of you gets in any more trouble in this town, I'll not only lock you up, I'll throw away the key!"

Outside the restaurant where Jessie and Ki were seated at a table near the door, dusk was turning into darkness.

"I heard you talking to Hayes," Ki said. "Were you really going to hire a lawyer to dig up any dirt he could on the marshal?"

"To tell you the truth, Ki, that was a bluff on my part," Jessie answered, forking a piece of roast ham into her mouth. "But once I started on it, I didn't want to let it go."

"Oh? Why not?" Ki finished devouring the beefsteak and fried potatoes he had ordered.

"It was Hayes himself who intrigued me—I should say Hayes's response to my bluff about hiring a lawyer. He went as stiff as a stick. He looked, in a word, scared. It made me wonder if perhaps there really might be something about him or his past or maybe his relationships here in town that he didn't want known. Why else would he act so worried about a lawyer looking into his background?"

"Most people have things in their past that they wouldn't want the world to know about."

"I agree. But, as I said, the marshal was on the edge—I won't say of panic—but certainly of fear. Maybe I really should hire a lawyer to look into the life and times of Buck Hayes."

"Don't waste your time," Ki advised. "We have other fish to fry."

"Like Arthur Reese, you mean."

"Also Addison Chaney and Lon Curlew. How'd your interview with Chaney go? You did get to see him?"

"I saw him. But I got nowhere with him. The man was righteously indignant to think that I would dare to inquire into his business dealings. He insisted he had a mortgage on the Latrobe homestead but, when I asked to see it, he refused to show it to me."

"I had pretty much the same experience with Curlew," Ki remarked.

"Opal told me that her father told her that Curlew demanded he arrest you on the charges of trespassing and disturbing the peace."

"That's right. Jessie, the whole thing smelled to high heaven. First of all, according to Curlew, Reese told Marshal Hayes that you and I had been questioning him this afternoon. Reese, Hayes claimed, sent him to see Curlew just in case we should decide to interview him. When Hayes showed up, Curlew did his little dance and the marshal hauled me off to jail."

119

"Very neat."

"Too neat."

"You think Hayes was out to get you—or me?"

"Sure, I do. Reese didn't like us coming to see him for some reason. So he enlists the long arm of the law to go looking for us to see if there's a way we can be encouraged to back off."

"You think that's why Hayes jailed you?"

Ki nodded and drank some of his tea. "We weren't causing any trouble for anyone when we talked to Reese, and yet he called in the law to track us down. Reese's goal was to intimidate us which, he probably thought, would make us back off. Make us want to stop asking questions about Mr. Latrobe's business dealings before his death with the powers that be here in El Paso."

"It sounds plausible," Jessie commented thoughtfully as she finished the last of her roast ham. "But I have to say, Ki, that a lawyer would be hard-pressed to prove your theory in a court of law."

"I admit I'm guessing. But Reese's reaction to our visit seems to me to be the last one a person would expect un-less—"

"Unless somebody somewhere has something to hide," Jessie interrupted.

Ki pointed an index finger at her and nodded. "You hit the nail right on the head."

"Well, so far we've not done very well in trying to sub-stantiate Tess's belief that Brent did not commit suicide. I hate to say this but the fact is I'm beginning to believe he did. I think he did because he was so deeply in debt that he could no longer face the mess he had gotten himself into. He did, after all, cash those two drafts Reese gave him."

"You may be right. There's no getting around the fact that Mr. Latrobe did borrow money—twice—from Reese. What I'd like to know is why were both Chaney and Curlew so reluctant to confirm Mr. Latrobe's indebtedness to them."

"Maybe they have no real evidence of such indebtedness as Reese did."

"Maybe not. That would explain why both men suddenly got their dander up when we went to ask about their dealings with Mr. Latrobe. Even going so far, in Curlew's case, to having me arrested on what were obviously trumped-up charges."

"Maybe we should have a look at the business records kept by Messrs. Chaney and Curlew as they relate to Brent Latrobe."

"But they're not going to show them to us," Ki protested. "We've already asked to see them and we were both turned down."

"I'm not talking about *asking* to see the records," Jessie said.

"You're talking about—"

"Taking the bull by the horns, so to speak, and—"

"Would you like some dessert, miss, sir?" asked the waiter who suddenly appeared at the table.

Jessie ordered apple pie. Ki ordered vanilla ice cream.

"When we've finished with dessert," Jessie said, "we'll break into Chaney's office and have ourselves a look around."

"Curlew's office is closer," Ki pointed out.

"Then we'll start there and move on to Chaney's office."

After leaving the restaurant, Jessie and Ki made their way to Curlew's darkened office where they waited for the street to be momentarily empty of passers-by. When it was, they slipped into the alley that separated the building from a tin shop on the opposite side of the alley. They moved through the thick shadows like shadows themselves, silent, almost invisible as they kept close to the wall of the building.

In the rear of the building, they tried the back door which was, as they had expected it to be, locked. A window next to the door on the ground level was also locked.

"Can you force the door?" Jessie asked in a low voice.

"I could," Ki replied. "But it would make some noise. And to break the window would make more. Wait here."

Jessie watched as Ki ran the palms of his hands along the boards that composed the facade of the building. She continued watching, amazed as always at the esoteric skills of her friend, as Ki began to climb the sheer wall of the building. His fingers found purchase in places Jessie could barely believe would provide a fly a handhold.

Ki made his way up the building with surprising speed until he reached the second floor window that had been his goal. He tried it. Then he spoke two words in the darkness that were just loud enough for Jessie to hear: "It's open."

She saw him slide the window sash up and then climb inside the building. She looked around. There was no one in sight. The area was quiet. She began to wonder if Ki had decided to search the office by himself. She was beginning to feel left out when she heard the inside bolt of the ground floor door being drawn back.

The door swung open. She caught her breath as a hand reached out, seized her arm, and quickly drew her inside.

Ki closed the door behind her and bolted it.

They made their way, Ki in the lead, through the back room and on into the office that Ki had been in earlier that day. He moved like a jungle animal—half-crouching, silently, and with surprising speed considering the almost total darkness. Jessie followed close behind him, only once bumping her hip on a piece of furniture that she could not see in the darkness.

"We need light to see by," she whispered when Ki halted.

As if her words had been a command, a small flame flared to pierce the darkness.

Ki lifted the globe of a coal oil lamp and held the match he had taken from the cuff of his jeans to it. Then he picked up a thick ledger that sat on Curlew's desk. He opened it and ran a finger down the pages that were filled with neatly inked notations. He hastily flipped through page after page.

"There's nothing here," he said finally. "This is just a list of sales and purchases of cattle."

"This might be something," Jessie said from the other side of the room. She held up an oblong wooden box she had found inside a tin cabinet. "But it's padlocked."

"Give it to me."

She handed the box to Ki. He shook it. "There are papers inside this," he said. "Paper money maybe."

"Not money," Jessie said. "Curlew would keep any money he has in that safe over there."

Ki placed the box in the center of Curlew's desk and stepped back. His breathing slowed, then quickened. He raised his right hand. His fingers were touching one another. He held his hand in a parallel plane with the walls of the room on his right and left. He raised his hand still higher and then he brought it down in one swift chopping motion.

The lid of the box split under the blow he had given it. The padlock fell on the desk. Ki removed the broken lid as Jessie moved closer to him and together they began to go through the documents the box contained.

There were land leases, Curlew's last will and testament, and assorted legal papers relating to his business.

In the midst of the mass of documents, Jessie found what they had been looking for but with no sense of triumph. Instead, a feeling of despair overcame her as she studied the two-page legal document that was clearly a mortgage on the Latrobe ranch. It was payable, the document stated, in regular monthly payments and, should the mortgagor default on the payments due, the mortgagee had the right to foreclose on the property in question. Jessie flipped to the next page and examined the bottom line where she saw Brent Latrobe's signature as mortgagor next to the signature of Lon Curlew, the mortgagee. Turning again to the first page, she quickly read through the document that stated in the event of the mortgagor's death, the instrument in question would become a lien on the estate of the deceased.

Jessie dropped the mortgage into the box. "That does it," she said. "Brent signed that document. That's his signature on it."

"You're sure?"

"Yes. Now let's get out of here."

"Do you think we should take the mortgage document with us to show Mrs. Latrobe?"

Jessie shook her head. "Curlew will be showing it to her soon enough, I expect."

Ki was about to blow out the lamp when he heard the sound of a key turning in a lock. "Somebody's coming!" he warned Jessie. "Get out the back way."

He gave her a push as the front door swung open and Curlew and Marshal Hayes, the latter with a six-gun in his hand, stormed into the office.

Jessie ran for the back door but Ki, in his haste to follow her, stumbled and fell against a heavy Morris chair.

Before he could regain his feet, Hayes was standing over him, his gun aimed at Ki's chest, Curlew at his side with his cane held in his right hand. "Mr. Curlew was on his way to his office just now to do some after-hours work," Hayes said bluntly. "When he spotted light leaking through the curtains on the front window, he came and got me."

"It's a good thing I did," Curlew muttered. "This miscreant might have killed me if I'd dared come in here alone to see what he was up to."

"On your feet," Hayes ordered Ki who was relieved to hear the bolt of the rear door being drawn.

"Buck, there's somebody in the back." Curlew cried. "There may be a whole gang of them!"

"Go see who it is," Hayes said.

But before Curlew could make a move, Ki arched his back, his right leg flew up and the gun in Hayes's hand flew toward the ceiling.

"God *dammit!*" the marshal muttered as Curlew drew back from Ki in alarm.

Ki got up on his hands and knees. Supporting himself on both palms, he extended his left leg, pivoted on his right knee while using his hands to maintain his balance, and swung his left leg in a sharp arc, knocking Hayes's legs out from under him.

The marshal went down hard, cursing all the way until he hit the floor. The wind was knocked out of him, which effectively silenced him.

Ki sprang up and made a run for it. But he never got into the back room. Something hit him on the back of his head, and he went down in a flurry of papers. The strong box, he thought. Curlew must have thrown it at me. A white light rioted through his mind, blinding him. His knees gave way and he fell to the floor.

"Get up!"

Ki recognized Buck Hayes's voice. It seemed to come to him from a great distance. He blinked dazedly up at the gun in the lawman's hand. Curlew's diversionary move with the strong box, Ki thought, gave Hayes time to recover from the dragon-tail kick I gave him. Ki rose slowly,

125

the movement intensifying the pain that was threatening to split his skull.

"Hands up!" Hayes ordered, gesturing angrily with his revolver.

Ki obeyed the order. He stood with his hands raised in front of Hayes. Curlew left the room, cane in hand, and then quickly returned. "There was someone else here, but they got out the back way," he told Hayes. "The door's open back there."

Ki was relieved to learn that Jessie had made good her escape.

When Hayes glanced at Curlew, Ki formed his left arm into the *chudan,* or middle block, position. Swinging his arm, he struck the wrist of Hayes's gun hand. But this time the marshal apparently had a stronger grip on his gun because he did not drop it.

Instead he rammed its barrel into Ki's gut, doubling Ki over and making him a perfect target for Curlew. The stockman brought his cane down hard on the back of Ki's head, sending him whirling down into a deep sea of total blackness.

Chapter 9

Ki awoke to familiar surroundings—the jail cell Hayes had placed him in after the first encounter with Curlew in the stockman's office. Now, here he was in it again after last night's encounter with Curlew and Hayes in the very same office.

He sat up somewhat groggily, the pain in his skull still rampant from where Curlew had struck him. He bent over, placing his head in his hands. Outside the window of his cell, on the branch of a sycamore tree, a wild canary sang. Its shrill song seemed to sharpen the pain Ki was experiencing.

He listened for sounds from the office beyond the closed door. He heard none. Was that because his mind was so addled with the pain of the blow he had suffered, he wondered. Or was the office empty?

Time passed.

The canary went winging away. Silence now outside as well as inside the jail. Ki's stomach rumbled with hunger.

More time passed.

Ki stood up as he heard the sound of the front door

being opened. "Hey!" he yelled and winced at the pain his shout had sent shooting through his skull. Bracing himself and gingerly massaging the spot on the back of his head where he had been struck by Curlew, he yelled again, "Hey!" This time the pain wasn't so bad. I'll live, Ki thought wryly. I will if I can get something to eat.

As if in answer to his thoughts, the door to the cell area opened to reveal Opal Hayes, a tray covered with a red and white checkered napkin in her hand.

"I don't know if I'm happier to see you, honey," Ki said, "or that tray which, I presume, is my breakfast."

"Well, I like that!" Opal exclaimed, prettily pretending pique. "I should think it would be definitely me you were happier to see."

She bent down and slid the tray through the narrow slot between the bars and the floor.

Ki picked it up, ripped off the napkin, and proceeded to devour the scrambled eggs, salt pork, and brown bread it held, not bothering with the knife and fork Opal had provided but using his fingers instead.

"Some men have absolutely no manners," Opal huffed.

"Fingers were invented before forks," Ki said around the food filling his mouth.

"Some men also haven't got the sense God gave geese." Opal added.

"I take it you mean me."

"I thought you would have learned your lesson by now. But papa says he caught you in Mr. Curlew's office and the charge is breaking and entering plus attempted robbery, resisting arrest, and—"

"I plead guilty."

"Ki, whatever possessed you to do such a thing?"

"I told you. Jessie and I promised Mrs. Latrobe we'd look into her husband's business dealings with various men in town before his death. Mrs. Latrobe doesn't believe her

128

husband committed suicide. But Jessie and I thought Mr. Latrobe might have committed suicide because of mounting debts."

"Well, did he?"

"So far as we can tell at this point—yes, it looks that way."

"Papa says you had a confederate. Was it Miss Starbuck?"

"My lips are sealed. I'm no snitch that tells tales out of school."

"Papa says Mr. Curlew wants Miss Starbuck arrested too. On suspicion of breaking and entering—"

"I know, I know. Attempted robbery and so on. What else does your papa say?"

"He says no amount of money in the world is going to bail you out of here this time."

Ki groaned. He had been expecting Jessie to show up at the Marshal's office to bail him out once again. "Where is your papa? Shouldn't he be here tending to business?"

"He had to go see Mr. Reese. Mr. Reese sent for him very early this morning—just as the sun was rising, as a matter of fact. Did you hear about the tragic accident that took place last night? No, of course you didn't since you spent the night locked up in here."

"What happened?"

"Mr. Charles Tremayne died. He fell off his horse and broke his neck. I suppose some people would say it serves him right for being drunk and disorderly but I wouldn't. I've committed enough sins in my time"—Opal gave Ki a sly wink—"to know better than to cast the first stone. Or even the second or third ones, for that matter."

Charles Tremayne. The name seemed familiar to Ki. At first, he couldn't place it. But then he remembered. Charles Tremayne had spoken to Tess Latrobe at the graveside service for Brent Latrobe. He was a good friend of the Latrobes, Ki recalled.

"Mr. Tremayne got drunk, I suppose, because of all the money he lost at poker last night to Mr. Reese and that tinhorn gambler, Jack Radcliff."

"And then he fell off his horse."

"Yes, that's what Mr. Roark said when he came to the house to fetch papa for Mr. Reese. Mr. Roark works for Mr. Reese. He said Mr. Tremayne was soused up, down, and sideways by the time he left the poker table. Mr. Roark also said that Mr. Tremayne signed over all his real estate holdings to Mr. Reese to whom he lost all he owned. But Mr. Roark said that Mr. Tremayne said he had some sort of business deal going on in the East and he claimed he would be able to redeem the IOU he gave Mr. Reese in a few days or a week at the most. It's a pity he died before he could do that. But drink and gambling have been the ruin of many a good man, sad to say."

"So has falling off a horse."

"Yes, that too. But Mr. Tremayne wouldn't have fallen off his horse if he hadn't been drunk and maybe distraught over his gambling losses." Opal sighed. "Well, now he's at the coroner's office, having escaped this vale of tears and gone to a happier life in heaven. He has, that is, if God doesn't hold his drunkenness and gambling against him."

"Opal, I've got to get out of here," Ki said, his thoughts racing, his worries about Jessie's safety—and his own—rising.

"I told you papa said he would accept no bail this time. Oh, Ki, I wish you had behaved yourself. I hate to see you in a predicament like this."

"Then help me."

"Help you? How?"

"Get the key to this cell door and let me out."

"Let you—" Opal recoiled in shock, one hand flying up

130

to cover her mouth that had opened in a shocked O.

"I sincerely believe I might be in danger if I remain here," Ki said. "I think Jessica might also be in danger. I've got to go to her."

"Danger? Whatever do you mean?"

"No questions now, honey. There isn't time. Just let me out."

"Ki, I don't dare do that. Papa would skin me alive if I let you escape."

"Honey, I thought we were good friends. Have you forgotten the good time we had in that hotel at Indian Junction?"

"No, I haven't forgotten."

"I'd hoped we'd have more times like that, you and me."

Opal began to shake her head. Slowly at first, then vigorously. "No," she said. "No, no, *no!*"

Ki pleaded with her as persuasively as he could. To absolutely no avail. Opal was adamant. Her papa would kill her. People would talk. They would wonder why she had let Ki escape. They would snicker and say that she had been seduced by the prisoner. She would never ever again be able to hold her head high in polite society. No, she simply could not do it.

Ki listened to her tirade. He tried to think of some way to persuade her to release him when she suddenly cried. *"Eureka!"*

Eureka? What was this eureka business?

"You became sick," Opal exclaimed dramatically. "You rolled about on the floor of your cell. You were gagging. I had to do something. There wasn't time to run for Doctor Swinton. So I opened the cell door, intending to try to clear your air passages with my fingers, to stop you from gagging—in order to save your life. But you sprang up and seized me! You had deceived me. You weren't sick at all.

131

You overpowered me. You tied me up. Then you made your escape, leaving me bound—you'd better gag me too, Ki so I can't scream—and so ends this sad story of a woman betrayed by still another scoundrel. Wait here, Ki. I'll get the key to the door. And some rope."

Wait here? Where did Opal think he was going?

She was back in a minute. She unlocked the door. She handed a coil of rope to Ki.

He began to tie her to the bunk. "The rope's not too tight, is it?" he asked her solicitously.

"No, it's fine. Hurry, Ki. Before papa or someone else comes."

Ki hurried.

Soon Opal was securely, if rather loosely, tied and gagged with the decorative lace handkerchief she told Ki to unpin from her dress and put to better use.

"I can't thank you enough for doing this for me, Opal," he said. "I hope to have the chance to repay your kindness."

As Ki bent and kissed her on the forehead, Opal mumbled something behind her gag. Ki thought he could guess what it was because she nudged his groin with her knee.

When Ki returned to the Latrobe ranch, he found Jessie in the barn saddling a buckskin mare. She was wearing jeans, a fringed deerskin jacket, and a man's cotton shirt.

"Ki!" she cried as he led his mount into the barn. "I was just on my way to town to—"

"Bail me out," Ki guessed.

"That's right. But you're free. What happened?"

Ki put his horse in a stall and filled a feed bin with oats for the animal. "I had a little help from a friend."

"A friend?" Jessie looked at him quizzically.

"Opal Hayes. She hatched a little scheme and I went along with it. She's tied up in my jail cell. I'm supposed to have tricked her into entering the cell. Then I'm supposed to have jumped her, tied her up, and made good my escape. It was all Opal's idea, bless her soul."

"They'll be after you. The marshal. A posse maybe."

"No doubt. I'll have to lie low until we're ready to leave here. By the way, Jessie, you'll probably have to do the same. Curlew heard you leaving his office last night. He didn't see you, but he suspects it was you. Marshal Hayes, according to Opal, intends to arrest you on suspicion of having broken into Curlew's office with me."

"How are we going to stay one step ahead of the law and still get done the job we set out to do for Tess?"

"Have you told her about the mortgage we found in Curlew's strong box?"

"No. She was asleep when I got back here last night. I didn't want to wake her. She was still asleep this morning when I got up and came out here. But the fact is I could have awakened her and told her the bad news about Brent having signed that mortgage that Curlew's got on the homestead. I just didn't want to face her with that fact, to tell you the truth."

"I don't blame you. She'll take it hard, coming as it does right on top of those two drafts you showed her concerning the loans Reese made to Mr. Latrobe."

"Well, now that you're back and I don't have to go into town to try to bail you out of jail, I guess I have no more excuses left to avoid giving Tess the bad news."

"I have two questions I want to ask Mrs. Latrobe. You ready to go in?"

Once inside the ranch, they found Tess sitting in a Queen Anne chair in the common room sipping coffee from a delicate china cup. She smiled when she saw them.

Jessie proceeded to tell Tess about the break-in at Curlew's office the night before and the finding of the mortgage signed by Brent Latrobe in Curlew's strong box.

When Jessie finished speaking, Tess looked out the window without saying anything at first. Her coffee cup clattered faintly against its saucer as the hand holding it began to tremble slightly.

After a long moment, Tess squared her shoulders, steadied her hand, and turned to face Jessie and Ki again.

"I am a foolish old woman," she told them in a resigned voice. "I should never have bothered you both about this matter of Brent's death—the terrible form it took. I should have made myself face the facts. I should have had the courage to face up to the fact that Brent, for whatever reasons, managed to fall heavily into debt, and in the end, the burden was simply too much for the poor man to bear. I am obliged to ask you both to forgive me for troubling you."

"It was no trouble," Jessie said. "I'm sorry, Tess, that things didn't turn out differently for you."

"If I may," Ki said quietly, "I'd like to ask you some questions, Mrs. Latrobe."

"Of course, Ki."

"Do you know anything about a man named Roark who, I understand, is employed by Arthur Reese?"

Tess made a sour face. "A good-for-nothing, that man. Perhaps worse. A man of ill-repute."

"Mrs. Latrobe, have you heard any talk about Roark, acting on behalf of Arthur Reese, having hired some men to run-off settlers in these parts, and Addison Chaney putting their land up for sale at public auction when they had fled and subsequently failed to make their mortgage payments?"

"Yes, I did hear something about that a few months back. People were not willing to say too much or be too specific at the time, as I recall. Brent told me he had the impression that it had been a bad business. Arthur, of course, denied having any part in the incident in which, I'm sorry to say, a pregnant woman was killed by the mar-

134

auders. Arthur dismissed the whole thing as a drunken spree by some anonymous drifters that got out of hand. Nothing was ever proved one way or the other."

"Speaking of drunken sprees, that leads me to my next question. Have you heard Mrs. Latrobe, about Charles Tremayne's unfortunate accident?"

"Charles has had an accident? Oh, dear, what happened to him? Is he badly hurt?"

"I'm afraid he's dead, Mrs. Latrobe," Ki said solemnly, wishing that he could, just once, bring this poor woman a piece of good news.

"Dead?" Tess repeated, the word echoing dismally in the quiet room.

"The story is that he got drunk and fell off his horse following a poker game."

"Charles drunk?" Tess looked stunned.

"I'm sorry, Tess," Jessie said, going to the woman and placing a comforting hand on her shoulder. "I know Charles Tremayne was a good friend of yours and Brent's."

"No," Tess said, shaking her head. "It can't be. Are you sure it was Charles Tremayne who had the accident, Ki?"

"I have it on rather good authority—from the marshal's daughter. She told me her father had learned about the accident early this morning from the man named Roark."

"I have to tell you something," Tess said. "I've known Charles for nearly fifteen years. In all of that time, I have never known him to take a drink. Not once. Why, he has belonged to the Temperance Union ever since I've known him. Charles may have fallen off his horse and been killed, but I can guarantee you he was not drunk when the accident happened, not Charles Tremayne."

"There's something else, Mrs. Latrobe, that I think I should mention to you. I heard from Opal Hayes that Roark informed her father that Mr. Tremayne had lost all

135

his money and also extensive real estate holdings during the poker game he was involved in before his accident. He lost them to Arthur Reese."

Jessie thought she saw something unspoken pass between Tess and Ki.

"It wasn't an accident," Tess breathed finally, still staring hard at Ki.

"Opal also told me," he continued, "that Mr. Tremayne mentioned, at the poker game, I suppose, that he had business interests in the east from which he could obtain the means to redeem the real estate he had pledged to Reese in the form of an IOU. But he died before he could reclaim his lands.

"There is, too, a certain similarity between Mr. Tremayne's death and the death of your husband, Mrs. Latrobe," Ki continued. "The former dies in a fall right after placing himself deeply in debt to Arthur Reese. Your husband commits suicide after placing himself deeply in debt to Arthur Reese, Addison Chaney, and Lon Curlew."

"A coincidence?" Jessie asked as much of herself as of anyone else in the room.

"Possibly," Ki said.

"Unlikely," a suddenly strong-voiced Tess stated flatly.

"Opal Hayes told me that three men were involved in the poker game," Ki said. "Mr. Tremayne, of course. Arthur Reese. And a man named Jack Radcliff."

"I have heard of Radcliff," Tess said with distaste. "A professional gambler and not an entirely honest one, or so I've been told."

"Do you know where we might find this Jack Radcliff so we could have a talk with him?" Ki asked Tess.

"He's usually at the Empire Saloon I'm told, plying his dubious trade," Tess answered. "That's on Alamo Avenue."

"I think we should talk to Radcliff as soon as possible, Jessie," Ki said.

"I agree. Let's go."

As they were about to leave the ranch, they heard the jingling of harness as a wagon pulled up outside and there was a knock on the door. A white-coated servant answered the door and then announced the arrival of a Mr. Richard Defoe to see Mrs. Latrobe.

"I don't know the gentleman," Tess responded, "but please show him in."

A moment later, a tall, thin man wearing round spectacles entered the room, blinking as his eyes grew accustomed to the room's relatively dim interior after the bright sunlight outside. In his hand was a bulging leather briefcase.

"Mr. Defoe," Tess said, rising, "I'm Mrs. Latrobe. You wanted to see me?"

"Ah, yes, Mrs. Latrobe." Defoe crossed the room, took Tess' hand, and shook it. "I want to take this opportunity to express my heartfelt sorrow for your loss. I share Governor Kirkland's feelings of deep regret over the lamentable loss of Mr. Latrobe."

"You must be the special prosecutor I asked the governor to send to investigate my husband's death."

"You're quite correct, Mrs. Latrobe. I am an employee of the state's attorney general's office. I've come to make an appointment with you, Mrs. Latrobe, to discuss the matter that concerns you. When would you find it convenient to—"

"Right now, Mr. Defoe. If, of course, that's all right with you."

"Yes, perfectly all right."

"Let me introduce you to two friends of mine who also have, at my urgent request, been looking into the matter. May I present Miss Jessica Starbuck and her friend and

137

colleague, Ki. Jessie, Ki—Mr. Richard Defoe."

Jessie and Ki shook hands with Defoe and then Tess urged them to summarize for Defoe what they had found out so far.

They did so, each of them taking turns recounting the various events and discoveries of the past few days. Ki concluded by telling Defoe what he had heard about the accidental death of Charles Tremayne.

"Very interesting," mused Defoe when Ki had finished speaking. "I gather from your tone and manner of speaking, Ki, that you think Mr. Tremayne's death may not be quite what it appears to be."

"Let's say I think it bears looking into, Mr. Defoe," Ki responded. "In fact, Jessie and I were just going into El Paso to see what more we might be able to find out about the incident when you arrived."

"You're perfectly welcome to come with us, Mr. Defoe," Jessie said.

"I'm sure it would be a most interesting experience, Miss Starbuck. But I think I would do well to confer first at greater length with Mrs. Latrobe about her husband and the months preceding his death. I would also like to look if I may, madam, at the business records of this ranch."

"I'll get them for you, Mr. Defoe," Tess said, "and I'll gladly answer all your questions."

"Tess, we'll be back—well, when you see us," Jessie said.

Tess went to Jessie and the two women embraced. She took Ki's hand in both of her own and said, "Both of you, be careful. I would never forgive myself if something happened to either one of you."

Jessie and Ki rode down Alamo Avenue in El Paso, and when they arrived in front of the Empire Saloon, they dismounted and wrapped their horses' reins around a hitchrail next to a wooden water trough.

Once inside the saloon, they surveyed the nearly empty room. There were two men engaged in bawdy conversation with a tired-looking woman, who was wearing even more tired-looking finery consisting mostly of feathers and false jewels. Another man snored in a corner beneath one of the tables. At the bar, a hulking figure of a man was talking earnestly to the bar dog.

"None of these men look like what I imagine Jack Radcliff would look like," Jessie said.

"Let's ask the bar dog if he's here," Ki suggested.

They made their way to the bar in time to hear the man who was talking to the bar dog say, "You swear you don't know where Radcliff is?"

The bar dog, rolling his black eyes heavenward and raising his right hand, intoned, "I swear I don't and may the Lord strike me dead if I lie. I haven't laid an eye on Radcliff since the poker game broke up early this morning."

"I want you to do something for me," the man at the bar said. "I want you to send word to me right away if Radcliff comes in here. I got to talk to him about something important. You got that?"

"I got it," said the nervous bar dog.

When the other man had gone barreling through the batwings, Jessie said, "I guess then that we too are out of luck."

"Ma'am?"

"We came in here looking for Jack Radcliff too," Ki explained.

"Who might you two be?"

"I'm Jessica Starbuck and this is a friend of mine, Ki."

"I haven't ever heard of you, mister," the bar dog said, "but I sure have heard of you, Miss Starbuck. I used to

139

work for your daddy's freight line when I was a young man out in the California gold fields. I'd gone out there to see the elephant, but I caught nary a glimpse of him. Had to take a job when I couldn't hit pay dirt. It's a small world, ain't it?"

"Do you know where we might look for Mr. Radcliff?" Jessie asked.

"Sure, I do. He's in the outhouse out back. He had himself a real snootfull last night, Jack did. That poker game went on for hours and hours and hours. He went to the outhouse afterward and, by golly, didn't he fall asleep out there. Good thing it's a four-seater."

The bar dog guffawed, holding his prominent belly in both hands.

"But you told that man who was just here that you didn't know where Radcliff was," Ki said, puzzled.

"That fellow—you know him?"

Ki shook his head.

"You're better off not knowing him. What a man don't know won't hurt him, folks say. Anyway, that was Roark. He don't have any other name, far as I know. He's a holy terror sober or drunk, awake or asleep. I don't know what he wants with Jack, but whatever it is, I'm not about to put him on Jack's trail. Roark, come to think of it, does have another name. It's Trouble."

"I understand he works for Arthur Reese," Ki said.

"And for anyone else with who wants dirty work done and is willing to pay for it—but don't you quote me on that."

"I'll go out and wake up our Mr. Radcliff," Ki said to Jessie.

"What'll you have, Miss Starbuck?" the bar dog asked. "It's on the house."

Not wanting a drink, but also not wanting to offend the

man who had been so helpful, Jessie ordered Old Pepper burbon with water. She was sipping the drink when Ki returned with a mustached man of about fifty, whose checkered coat and silk vest were slightly askew but whose derby was perched at a rakish angle on his handsome head.

"Ah, you must be Miss Jessie Starbuck," said the man, doffing his hat and bowing. "I have heard of you, Miss Starbuck. Now, Lady Luck smiles on Jack Radcliff, and he has a chance to meet you in person."

"How do you do, Mr. Radcliff," Jessie said as Radcliff took her hand and planted a kiss upon it, his mustache tickling her as he did so.

"Ki, who roused me from the depths of Morpheus' arms, tells me you want to talk to me about last night's poker game."

"Would you like something to drink, Mr. Radcliff?" Jessie asked.

"I don't mind if I do. Since I am, so to speak, off duty. Whiskey," Radcliff told the bar dog. "Neat. Hair of the dog, don't you know?"

The bar dog poured the drink and Radcliff quickly downed it, holding his eyes clamped shut as he did so as if he were imbibing hemlock. He set down the glass, sighed, patted his lips with a silk handkerchief, and asked, "What is it you wanted to know about last night's game?"

"You were playing with Mr. Reese and Mr. Tremayne, I believe, weren't you?" Jessie asked.

"Yes, I was. Astute player, Mr. Tremayne."

"Astute, you say?" Ki asked quickly. "But Mr. Tremayne, we were told, lost not only all his money but also his real estate holdings to Mr. Reese."

"Lost, you say? You have been talking to the wrong party, sir. You have been badly misinformed, sir. Mr. Tremayne practically cleaned me out. Mr. Reese as well. But

141

that is the way for men like me. We knights of the green cloth, as some call us, have learned to take the bitter with the sweet and last night was decidedly bitter for both me and Mr. Reese."

Ki stared in disbelief, first at Radcliff and then at Jessie. She said, "Ki, do you think Opal was mistaken when she told you that Charles Tremayne lost at poker last night?"

"I don't think so."

"Excuse me," Radcliff said. "Are you two talking about our marshal's fair young daughter?"

"Yes," Ki said. "She told me that a man named Roark told her father that Mr. Tremayne lost a great deal at cards last night."

"I think she must have been misinformed," Radcliff said. "Certainly, such a lovely young thing would not lie."

Ki excused himself and walked down to the end of the bar where the bar dog was waiting on a customer. When the man was finished, Ki asked him if he had been aware of the outcome of last night's poker game.

"Nope," said the bar dog. "Last night was a busy one. It kept me busier than a one-legged man in an ass-kicking contest. I never got out from behind the bar, and they were playing at a table down there by the door. Ask Jack. He'll tell you what happened."

"Thanks," Ki said and rejoined Jessie.

"And you say you haven't heard about Mr. Tremayne's sudden death last night?" Jessie was saying to Radcliff when Ki arrived at her side.

"Oh, my no, I haven't. I was, as I believe you know, indisposed during the wee hours of the morning after this establishment had closed its doors and good folk had gone home and tucked themselves into bed. Died, you say?"

"An accident, we've been given to understand," Ki said. "Mr. Tremayne fell off his horse and broke his neck."

142

"How awful." Radcliff hastily summoned the bar dog. "I need another drink. Make it a double."

When he had downed the drink, he turned back to Jessie and Ki and said mournfully, "Lady Luck is a fickle maiden. One moment she smiles on you, the next she turns her back on you. Poor Mr. Tremayne. A winner one minute; a loser the next."

"We thank you, Mr. Radcliff, for your time," Jessie said. "You've been very helpful."

"Please don't consider me insulting, Miss Starbuck," Radcliff said brightly, "but do you play poker?"

"Like a riverboat gambler," Ki interjected.

"Then maybe sometime—"

"Yes, maybe sometime, Mr. Radcliff," Jessie said. "Goodbye."

Outside on the boardwalk, Jessie said, "What in the world is going on here, Ki?"

"Something definitely is, but what? Well, we may be able to find out."

"Roark tells Marshal Hayes that Charles Tremayne lost everything to Arthur Reese last night and now one of the participants in that poker game tells *us* that Charles Tremayne *won* last night!"

"And Roark also told marshal Hayes that Mr. Tremayne fell off a horse—wait a minute. I'll be right back, Jessie."

Ki pushed through the batwings, leaving Jessie alone on the boardwalk. When he returned moments later, his face was grim.

"I forgot to ask Radcliff something," he said.

"Ask him what?"

"Opal told me that Roark had told her father that Mr. Tremayne was roaring drunk when he died."

"But Tess insisted he was not a drinking man."

"So I just asked Radcliff if Tremayne had had anything

143

to drink last night before, during, or after their poker game."

"What did he say?"

"He said Mr. Tremayne drank sarsaparilla all night long."

Chapter 10

Ki suddenly sensed something was wrong.

Then he realized what it was. He pulled Jessie back into the shadows shed by the saloon's overhang and pointed.

"Buck Hayes," she breathed, her eyes on the marshal who was standing diagonally across the street with his back to her and Ki.

"And Roark," Ki said, referring to the man to whom Hayes was talking. "We'd better get out of here before the marshal spots us. I don't fancy spending any more time in that jail of his."

"Move to the left," Jessie said. "Then we can come up on our horses with them between us and Hayes. That way, chances are he won't spot us if he turns around."

They moved to the left and then angled in toward their horses, which were tied to the hitchrail in front of the saloon.

They had almost reached their mounts when Jack Radcliff came jauntily through the Empire's batwings and started down the boardwalk toward them.

"Radcliff!"

It was Roark who had roared the gambler's name from across the street.

As Hayes turned around, Jessie and Ki ducked down and remained motionless a few feet from their horses.

Roark bounded off the boardwalk in the far side of the street and strode toward Radcliff who had halted and was watching the man approach.

"He's got a gun," Jessie said as she watched Roark continue advancing toward the gambler.

As Radcliff drew a derringer from beneath his coat, Ki observed, "So does Radcliff now."

"You'll never cheat me in another card game, Radcliff," Roark roared.

A shot shattered the stillness.

Smoke rose from the barrel of Roark's gun. He tilted the barrel upward and calmly blew the smoke away.

Radcliff clutched his chest, staggered backward, hit the front wall of the saloon, and then slid slowly down it, a stricken expression on his face.

Ki straightened up and moved out from behind the horses into Hayes's line of vision, ignoring the crowd that had gathered. "Marshal," he yelled, "that was cold-blooded murder. Roark killed Radcliff without giving the man a chance to defend himself."

Jessie joined Ki. "He's right, Marshal. So why are you just standing there? Arrest him." She pointed at Roark.

Hayes ambled across the street and took up a position next to Roark. "Arrest Mr. Roark?" Hayes asked. "For shooting a man in self-defense?"

"In cold blood!" Ki shouted.

"He drew first," Roark said with a nod in the direction of the dead gambler.

"That's not true," Jessie said. *"You* drew first. But even if Radcliff had drawn first he couldn't have killed you with that derringer of his. He couldn't have even wounded you because you were way beyond his gun's range."

"But Radcliff wasn't out of range of your revolver." Ki pointed out.

"Why haven't you arrested Roark?" an angry Jessie hotly asked Hayes.

"If there's any arrests to be made here today, it's you two who will be arrested for breaking and entering and a whole host of other charges," Hayes answered. "Now, are you two going to come along nice and peaceful or are Mr. Roark and I going to have to shoot the pair of you?"

Roark, when Hayes mentioned his name, aimed his gun directly at Ki.

Hayes's six-gun cleared leather and was aimed at Jessie.

"I don't believe this is happening," Jessie muttered to Ki. "Let's get our horses and make a run for it."

She lunged for her mount. As she swung into the saddle, Roark fired a shot that missed her but spooked Ki's horse. The horse ripped its reins free of the hitchrail and went galloping madly down the street and quickly disappeared.

Ki, as Jessie galloped rapidly away and then turned sharply onto a side street where she was lost to sight, threw himself to the ground before either Roark or Hayes could fire at him. He rolled over in a forward somersault and came up fast. He swung a stiff left arm which knocked Hayes' gun to the ground and then he threw his fisted right hand which caught Roark on the side of the head and sent the man toppling to the ground.

Ki turned and ran. He ziz-zagged down the street as people on the boardwalk gaped in amazement at him.

Behind him, a recovered Roark had retrieved his gun and gotten to his feet. He fired at Ki, a wild shot that missed its target by nearly a foot. Roark fired a second time, hitting a lamp post this time and causing one watching woman to scream and another one to faint.

Ki turned sharply and darted into an alley.

"After him!" he heard Hayes shout from somewhere behind him. A moment later, he heard the sound of running feet. He glanced back over his shoulder as he raced down the alley and saw Roark and Hayes in swift pursuit, with a crowd of townsmen running right behind them.

"Escaped prisoner!" Hayes yelled. "Let's get him, boys!"

Ki rounded the corner of the building at the end of the alley and started to run past the rear entrances of the stores. On his left was an open expanse of meadow. No place to hide there. Once the mob rounded the corner behind him, he knew, the shooting would start again.

He slowed down and tried a door. Locked. he tried the next one he came to. Also locked. Desperate, he looked behind him. Then ahead and above him.

He came to a halt and upended a rain barrel that sat beside one of the buildings. He climbed up on it and boosted himself up onto the overhang behind one of the stores. Flattening himself, he held his breath.

The mob of pursuing men came baying like hounds in heat out of the alley. From his perch on the roof, Ki could see them and the blood lust in their eyes. They halted, looking right and left for some sign of him. He was sure that if they discovered him, Roark would not hesitate to kill him as deliberately as he had just killed Jack Radcliff.

Ki didn't believe for a minute that Roark had killed Radcliff because, as Roark had claimed before gunning the gambler down, Radcliff had cheated him in a card game.

Ki, almost the instant the shooting occurred, had formed the theory that Arthur Reese might well have ordered Roark to kill Radcliff.

Why? That was easy. Reese certainly wouldn't want Radcliff going around town telling anyone who would listen that Charles Tremayne had not lost to Reese at poker but, on the contrary, had won. If people heard that after hearing Reese's conflicting claim about the outcome of the poker game that according to Reese left him, after Tremayne's death, the sole owner of Tremayne's extensive and lucrative real estate holdings, Reese could find himself in serious trouble.

Had Reese killed Tremayne? Ki didn't know, but he suspected such might be the case. Maybe Reese had arranged to have Tremayne killed and then spread the story about the "accident" that supposedly led to the man's death—a fall from his horse. But all this was mere speculation. Ki needed proof. He thought he knew of a way to get it.

The crowd milled about at the mouth of the alley, arguing about where Ki had gone and what to do next.

Hayes barked an order. Some of the men went one way. The rest, Hayes and Roark among them, headed in the direction of Ki's hiding place.

Ki pressed his body as flat as possible against the tarpaper on the overhang. He heard the men coming and then he heard them going beyond where he lay so still and silent. He remained motionless, listening to the sounds the men were making fade away. Then, after forcing himself to wait still longer, he warily raised his head and looked around.

There was no sign of his pursuers in either direction. He eased his body over the edge of the overhang, his legs dangling. When his feet made contact with the rain barrel, he let go of the overhang and jumped from the rain barrel down to the ground.

He started to trot back the way he had come, intending to make his way back along the alley that led to the business section of Alamo Avenue. Once there, he would have to get himself a horse so he could discover what had happened to Jessie.

He had almost reached the alley when several men strolled out of it, talking among themselves. Ki halted. So did the men. He stared at them. They stared at him. Then, as if someone had shouted an order, both Ki and the men sprang into action.

"That's him!" one of the men bellowed and lunged for Ki.

Ki dodged to one side. As a second man tried to grab him, he dropped to his right knee and, with a blow of his left arm, deflected the man's right arm. He slid forward along the ground, reached out, palms up, and clutched the man's sex organs which he squeezed as hard as he could.

His would-be attacker screamed in pain, but Ki maintained the hold he had gained as a result of his martial arts maneuver that was called Monkey Steals the Peach.

The other men, paralyzed by the sound of the screams ripping out of the throat of the man Ki had under control, were almost motionless.

Ki wasn't. He maintained his painful Monkey Paw hold and also seized his would-be attacker's chin with his free left hand. Then he lifted the man bodily and threw him into the crowd, knocking the men to the ground where they lay in a pile of helplessly flailing arms and legs.

He leaped over the tangle of bodies and sprinted down the alley and then out of it, almost getting run over in the middle of Alamo Avenue by a wagon loaded with farm implements. But he managed to make it safely to the other side of the street where he hesitated for a moment. Then, when the men led by Hayes and Roark appeared at the far end of the street, he looked around, desperately seeking a safe haven. There was none around that he could see. But suddenly he knew where to find one. He turned and ran, his heart pounding in his chest, his blood pounding in his head. He didn't stop until he reached his destination.

He tried the door of the house he finally reached and

it was closed. He tore it open, almost ripping it from its hinges, and dashed inside, slamming the door behind him. He stood with his back pressed against it, breathing heavily and sweating profusely.

In front of him stood a buxom woman in a low-cut gown of yellow satin that was trimmed with white lace. Her hands were on her hips and she was leering at Ki.

"What's the hurry, handsome?" she asked him. "Can't wait to make the two-backed beast with one of my girls?"

When Ki said nothing, the woman asked, "What's the matter, handsome? The cat got your tongue?"

Ki tried to speak but he couldn't because his throat was too dry and his chest was pumping like a blacksmith's bellows. Finally, with much effort, he managed to utter a name.

"Rosa," he gasped.

The woman in the yellow gown turned, cupped her hands around her mouth, and, in the voice of a teamster, yelled, "Come on downstairs, Rosa, honey. You've got a gentleman caller. And he looks like he's hot to trot so you hurry up, hear?"

By the time Rosa had come down from the second floor, Ki had regained his breath and his composure.

"Oh, it's you!" she cried with what seemed to Ki real pleasure.

"Hello, honey."

"This is Ki," Rosa told the woman in the yellow gown. "Ki, this is Mrs. Petry. She owns this establishment."

"Pleased to meet you, ma'am."

"Same here," said Mrs. Petry. "Well, I'll be on my way. You two enjoy yourselves."

Rosa took Ki by the hand and led him upstairs.

Once inside her room with the door closed, Ki sat down in a chair near the window.

Rosa stared at him. "Aren't you ready?"

"Not quite."

Rosa frowned. "Is something wrong?"

"I'm afraid there is, but it's a long story that would probably bore you to death."

"It's that Miss Starbuck, isn't it? Whatever's bothering you, Ki—and I can tell something is—it has to do with her, doesn't it?"

"Yes." Seeing the concerned look on Rosa's face as she sat down on the floor in front of him and took his hand, Ki said, "Jessie and I—we just had ourselves a little trouble here in town."

"I don't mean to pry, Ki. But if you want to tell me about it, I'll be glad to listen. I'll even try to help if there's any way I can."

Ki stroked her warm hand. He then bent forward and kissed her lightly on the lips.

He briefly described the shooting of Jack Radcliff. Then why he had been chased by Roark, Marshal Hayes, and a number of townsmen.

"I think you're right about the killing," Rosa said when he had finished. "Roark's a gunslick, and he'd sure enough know that Radcliff's derringer had no range at all to speak of. He was as safe as butter in a churn when he faced-off with Radcliff. Yep, it was cold-blooded murder, like you said."

"There's something wrong in this business of Tremayne's death. At the very least, Jack Radcliff's story of what happened in the poker game doesn't fit with the one Arthur Reese has been telling. Radcliff claimed Tremayne cleaned out both him and Reese. Reese claims Tremayne lost to him—just about everything the man owned, in fact, except his horse and the clothes on his back."

"I don't think you have to worry about Miss Starbuck like you say you've been doing, Ki. She got away clean, you said. She's probably gone somewhere to lie low until

152

she can hook up with you again. I envy her."

"I suppose a lot of people do. She's rich, she's young, she's—"

"Beautiful."

Ki nodded.

"I don't envy her because she's young or rich or even beautiful, for that matter. I envy her because she's got you for a good friend. Someone to stand by her when times are rough. Someone to lean on. Someone to worry about her. I've never had anybody like that, but I sure would like to have somebody like that."

"You'll find somebody someday, Rosa. A woman like you is bound to meet her match. It's just a matter of time."

"Till then," Rosa said mischievously, "I'll have as good a time as I can with any man who wants to lead me down the garden path. Aren't I awful?"

"On the contrary, I think you're wonderful."

Soberly, Rosa asked Ki if there was anything she could do for him. "Besides getting down to business in bed, I mean," she explained.

"There is something. Two things, actually. Would it be all right with you if I stayed here until dark? I don't want to leave while it's still daylight. Not with half of El Paso after me."

"That's fine with me. It will give us more time to get to know each other, even better than we did the first time you were here. But there's Mrs. Petry to consider. She's a business woman through and through. She'll want to be paid her share of my earnings for the time I spend with you. Tell you what, Ki. I'll only charge you half what I usually charge and I'll pay Mrs. Petry partly out of my own money, how's that?"

"I told you you were wonderful."

"You said there were two things I could do for you. What's the other thing?"

"The other thing is this. I want to pay a visit to the

coroner's office when I leave here after dark. I—"

"You can't."

"I can't?"

"His office closes at six o'clock and it won't be dark by then. If you go there when it is dark he'll be shut up tighter than a drum."

"That's fine with me."

It took a moment before comprehension dawned on Rosa. "You mean you intend to break into the coroner's office?"

"I do."

"But, Ki, whatever in the world for? All you'll find in the coroner's office is dead bodies."

"What's his name, the coroner?"

"Justin Bowdeen."

"Where's his office?"

"Number sixty River Street."

"Does he live at the same address?"

"No. His home's a block away—number eleven Austin Avenue."

"Thanks, honey."

"Anything else I can do for you?"

"There sure is."

"Don't tell me what it is. I think I can guess." Rosa let go of Ki's hand and began to unbutton his fly.

She reached inside his trousers and drew his already stiffening shaft out. She stroked it slowly, fanning the hot fire that had begun to burn in Ki while she was holding his hand. He watched her deftly manipulate his member until it was as stiff as a stone in her hand. Its head had begun to glisten, a sure sign of his arousal.

Rosa released her hold on him and eased his trousers down around his thighs. Now that his loins were completely exposed, she cupped his balls in her left hand. She gripped his shaft in her right hand and bent her head. Her lips parted and Ki watched his manhood disappear into the hot cavern of her mouth. He threw back his head as he felt her tongue begin to lave him all over.

Then, with her tongue forming a slippery velvet trough for his throbbing member to rest upon, she began to move her head rhythmically—up, then down, up again. The tempo of her movements slowly increased until they reached a rapid pace that brought Ki to the verge of a climax.

Just when he was sure he could not contain himself any longer, Rosa would change the speed of her movements or shift position slightly so that he was eased back from the exciting edge to which she had so skillfully taken him.

Then she would begin all over again. Her tongue licked him. Her lips embraced him. Her left hand caressed his balls. Her right, which now encircled the base of his shaft, jerked it maddeningly.

Ki gripped the arms of the chair in which he was sitting. he spread his legs. As he did so, Rosa released him and lowered her head even farther. He felt her tongue on his balls as her right hand continued to massage his pulsating manhood.

Rosa took his balls into her mouth. Her hand continued to work its wild magic on his shaft.

Moments later, he groaned, lost in a sweet land of ecstasy.

Rosa drew back and looked up at him. "Are you—"

"Yes," Ki muttered.

As she took him into her mouth again, he placed his hands on the back of her head. His pelvis began to move as if it had a will and life of its own.

When he came in Rosa's mouth, she gagged at first but then began to swallow. Her lips made soft sucking sounds as Ki's pelvis rose even higher and his hands pressed down on the back of her head.

Rosa continued sucking until Ki finally slumped down in his chair and sighed deeply. Then, as his hands fell away from her head, she let him go and sat back on her haunches. Looking up at him, she ran the back of one hand across her lips.

"It doesn't look like it wants to quit," she said.

Ki looked down at his manliness that seemed to paw the air as it jerked several times in quick succession. "That soldier can stand at attention for hours," he said, "and never get tired."

"You give a working girl a challenge, Ki," Rosa said teasingly. "What will it take to make your well run dry?"

For the next several hours, Rosa tried several different techniques until, at last, Ki's well did run dry. His soldier could no longer stand at attention. And he felt as if he could lick his weight in butterflies.

Then, as darkness settled on the land outside and Rosa lit a lamp, he pulled up his trousers and buttoned his fly.

"You're leaving?"

He nodded.

"You be careful, hear? You said yourself practically the whole town's on the lookout for you."

"I'll be careful."

"Good, I wouldn't want anything bad to happen to my best customer."

Ki paid Rosa, kissed her goodbye and then left Mrs. Petry's parlor house.

By the time Ki arrived at number sixty River Street, the darkness was complete, made so by the absence of a moon and by clouds that obscured the stars.

He stood in front of the coroner's office, nonchalantly leaning against the building as he idly picked his teeth with a wooden match stick he had taken from one of the rolled-up cuffs of his jeans. He waited until the street was almost empty and then discarded his makeshift toothpick. He reached behind him and tried the office door. It was locked as he had expected it to be. He edged away from the door toward a window just beyond it. That too turned out to be locked.

He walked down to the end of the block, turned left, and went to the entrance of the alley that ran behind the buildings fronting on River Street. He counted off the buildings as he walked until he was sure he was at the rear of the coroner's office.

He looked around him—there was no one in sight and no lamps burned in any of the nearby buildings. He tried the back door. Locked, like the front door. But not locked in the same way, he realized, because he had felt the door frame give ever so slightly when he had turned the knob.

He put his right shoulder against the door and pushed. Did the frame give a little bit? He pushed harder. Damn right it did! He stooped slightly and pushed against the door again. Then he straightened and, placing the palms of both hands against the door, he pushed against it.

The door was not locked with a key, he discovered as a result of his pushing against it in several different places. It didn't hold fast where the keyhole was but gave inward under pressure. It held fairly firm, however, at the level of Ki's shoulders. Which meant, he was certain, that the door was locked from the inside by some sort of bolt or, perhaps, a wooden bar. He hoped it was not the latter but even that might be made to give way if he gave it one or two karate kicks strong enough to dislodge the iron hinges that usually supported a blocking bar.

Ki pushed against the door at the level where he believed the bolt was. He heard a faint scraping of metal against metal. He pushed harder. A creaking sound met his ears as both wood and metal were placed under strain.

He pushed again, as hard as he could this time, and the door squeaked and something snapped.

Moving fast, Ki pushed the door open and stepped inside. The building was as black as the pit. He turned and closed the door. Feeling about in the darkness with his fingers, he located the hinge and the eye hook with which the door had been locked. The mechanism hung down along the side of the door, its other end having been torn free of the wall.

He stood without moving in the darkness, letting himself sense the contents of the room, letting his eyes learn to make out indistinct shapes as his night vision sharpened.

He was in a small room that contained a wood stove, a small table, and two wooden chairs. Several pots hung on hooks embedded in the wall. A coffee pot sat on the table. Ki felt it. Its contents were cold. He moved to the stove. No fire burned in it.

Moving cautiously, he went through an open archway that led to a large front room that apparently served as the coroner's office. It contained an open roll-top desk on which sat a lamp and a ledger, a free-standing coat and umbrella rack, and a couch covered in leather.

Ki picked up the lamp and lit it. Shielding its glow with one hand, he made for the door he had noticed on his right. He opened it and stepped into a room that was windowless. Taking his hand away from the lamp's smoky globe, he stared at the two tables, one on either side of the room, which were covered with white sheets. He glanced at the glass-fronted cabinets, the porcelain sink with its hand-operated pump, the bottles containing various substances, and the coil of rubber tubing that sat on a counter.

He turned his attention to the two tables. What—who —was under the white sheets?

He went to the one nearest to him and slowly drew back the sheet. He stared down at the lifeless body of Jack Radcliff who stared sightlessly back at him.

"Your dealing's over and done with for good old-timer," he said aloud to the gambler and then replaced the sheet.

He was crossing the room to the other table when he thought he heard a noise. He stopped and listened. This time he was sure he heard something and he was also sure of what it was he had heard. He had heard the metallic clatter of the broken bolt swinging back and forth as someone opened the rear door and entered the building. He hurriedly extinguished the lamp.

He thought of Marshal Buck Hayes and cursed his luck. He considered trying to make it back to the outer office. If he could manage that he might also manage to get out of the building somehow through the front door or window.

But before he could attempt to put his plan into action, he heard footsteps approaching the room in which he stood. He quickly ducked down under the table that held the mortal remains of Jack Radcliff and then he pulled the sheet covering the corpse down toward the floor in order to hide himself from view as the footsteps, coming closer, grew louder.

★

Chapter 11

Ki could see, seeping under the sheet behind which he had taken cover, a little light. Match, he thought. Then the light vanished and he heard a sharp intake of breath. Whoever it is just burned himself, he thought.

He heard a match being struck. Once again light pierced the utter blackness of the room. He got ready to make his move. His body tensed, his fingers flexed.

Footsteps. Coming closer. Light footsteps. Marshal Hayes? Ki began to doubt it was the lawman. The marshal would have had a much heavier tread. This intruder obviously had a lighter build than did Hayes. Was he becoming obsessed with Hayes? Ki asked himself. He didn't have time to seek the answer to his question because, whoever it was he was about to take down before making his escape from the coroner's office, was approaching the table beneath which he crouched.

The footsteps stopped.

The sheet covering the corpse of Jack Radcliff and shielding from sight the very much alive body of Ki was drawn slowly back . . .

Ki sprang upward, deliberately overturning the table on which Radcliff's corpse rested. As the match in the hand of the person he could not see went out, Ki seized the dark figure around the neck and began to squeeze. He ignored the pain of sharp fingernails clawing at his hand and arm as he continued to apply pressure.

Suddenly, he gasped, then gagged, as an elbow rammed backward into his gut. The wind was knocked from him and, as a result of the sneak attack, he momentarily loosened his grip on his opponent's throat.

A mistake. His arm was seized by strong hands. A moment later, Ki felt his feet leave the floor. He flew threw the air and landed with a crash some feet away on the floor at the foot of the table on which another lifeless body lay.

He was struggling to his feet when a voice snapped, "Don't move, I've got a gun and I'll use it."

Ki sank back down on the floor. He began to giggle.

"I mean it," the voice said angrily. "I'll shoot if you so much as sweat."

His giggling stopped finally. He caught his breath. "Don't shoot, Jessie," he said, "it's me."

There was a thick silence for several tense seconds and then the voice again—Jessie Starbuck's voice. "Ki? Is it really you?"

Ki took a match from the cuff of his jeans and lit it. He held it up to his face.

"What are *you* doing here?" Jessie exclaimed.

"My guess is that I'm here for the same reason you're here," Ki said.

"I came in the hope that Tremayne's body would still be here. I wanted to examine it."

"That makes two of us." Ki got to his feet, crossed the room, and relit the lamp. "It would appear that both of us wanted to confirm how Mr. Tremayne died and apparently

161

both of us decided the one fairly sure way to do that would be to examine his corpse."

"Is he here?" Jessie asked.

Ki pointed to the sheet-draped table.

Jessie moved toward it, returning her derringer to the pocket of her jacket.

"Hold it. Before you do that, let me ask you a question. Where'd you go when you rode out after that fracas with Roark and Radcliff this afternoon?"

"I rode a few miles out of town and holed up at a spring I found. I figured I'd come back when things cooled down some which I did. I went to the Empire Saloon and asked the bartender what had happened to you. He said he didn't know, but he did know that Hayes and the men with him had lost track of you. Where did you go?"

"I visited a lady friend of mine here in town. I stayed with her until it got dark and then I came here."

"I didn't know you knew anyone in town."

"Her name's Rosa Cortez." Ki moved closer to Jessie and held up the lamp. "Do you want to do the honors?"

Jessie drew back the sheet covering the body on the table.

"It's him," Jessie said softly.

"Charles Tremayne," Ki said as softly, remembering his one and only sight of the man at Brent Latrobe's graveside service when Tremayne had spoken briefly to Tess Latrobe. "Jessie, take the lamp, please."

When Jessie had done so, Ki stepped closer to the table and placed his hands on either side of Tremayne's neck.

"What are you doing?"

"Trying to find out whether the cause of death given by the coroner is the correct one."

"Can you do that with any certainty?"

As Ki's fingers gently prodded and probed, he nodded. "When I studied *Nien Jih Ssuch' u Chueh*—the Three Ways of the Death Touch, I also had to study human anatomy in order to learn how to inflict the Death Touch."

Ki withdrew his hands. "This man's neck has not been broken. Both the neck and the trachea are undamaged." He glanced at Jessie and then drew the sheet all the way down to expose all of Tremayne's naked body.

"Look at that!" Jessie said in a shocked tone.

Ki was looking at what she was referring to—the two small, almost neat bullet holes, one slightly above and to the left of the other, in Tremayne's upper chest.

Ki turned the rigid body on its left side. His action revealed the extensive damage done by the one bullet that had exited the body. The other, obviously, had remained within the man possibly deflected by a rib.

"The coroner lied about the cause of death," Jessie said.

"Maybe other people did too. People like Arthur Reese and Marshal Hayes. Tremayne didn't die from a fall from a horse. He never broke his neck. He was shot to death."

"By Arthur Reese," Jessie said. "So Reese could take possession of all the real estate Tremayne signed over to him in the IOU Tremayne wrote for Reese before he died."

"That's what it looks like," Ki agreed. "But we don't have any proof. It could have been somebody else who killed Tremayne. Somebody like Roark, Reese's hired gun."

"Maybe Roark was hired by Reese to kill Jack Radcliff to keep him from telling his version of the poker game?"

"The thought crossed my mind."

"Mine too."

"I think it's time we had a talk with Justin Bowdeen," Ki mused.

"Who's he?"

"The coroner."

"How'd you find out his name?"

"Rosa told me. She also gave me his office and his

163

home address. Which reminds me. How did you know where Bowdeen's office was?"

"I asked the bar dog at the Empire Saloon where I went just before I came here. He's a most obliging man and very free with information."

"Let's go, Jessie," Ki said after covering Tremayne's corpse. "I'm anxious to hear what Justin Bowdeen has to say to us about those bullet holes in Mr. Tremayne's body."

Ki pounded on the door of number eleven Austin Avenue as Jessie stood beside him, both of them impatiently awaiting a response from the occupant of the house.

It came a few minutes later. A man wearing a nightshirt opened the door, a lamp held high in his hand. He was of below average height and seemed even shorter because he had a tendency to stoop. His round-shouldered stance gave him the appearance of a man badly bent, if not deformed. His skin was sallow and had the texture of wax. His eyes were a pale gray that matched the color of the little hair he had left on his head.

"Who—what—" he began, peering uneasily at his nocturnal visitors.

"Are you Justin Bowdeen?" Ki asked.

"I am. And who, sir, are you and what do you mean by disturbing the peace of this house?"

Ki, followed by Jessie, pushed past Bowdeen and entered the house.

"What is the meaning of this?" an exasperated Bowdeen demanded to know. "How dare you break into my home in the middle of the night like this? *Who are you?*"

"My name is Ki. This is Miss Jessica Starbuck."

"Never heard of either one of you," snarled Bowdeen, the lamp wavering in his hand. "Never even saw either one of you. What do you want?"

"Information," Jessie said. "Information about the cause of Charles Tremayne's death."

"That's a matter of public record," Bowdeen declared officiously. "You may peruse the minutes of the coroner's inquest at the town hall. Now get out of my house, both of you before I send for Marshal Hayes to *get* you out of here!"

Ki, ignoring Bowdeen's threat, said, "We haven't got time to read the minutes of your inquest. Tell us what the findings were."

"This is highly irregular," Bowdeen protested.

Ki took a step closer to the coroner and said in a low voice, "If you don't start telling us what we want to know, Mr. Bowdeen, I'll get my dander up and then you'll really see how highly irregular things are going to get around here."

Bowdeen blanched.

"Ki has a terrible temper," Jessie said sweetly. "I'd do as he says if I were you."

Bowdeen did more than blanch at Jessie's words. He began to tremble. He braved a glance in Ki's direction.

Ki bared his teeth.

Bowdeen said, seeming to quote by rote from the inquest's minutes, "Cause of death in the case of Charles Tremayne was an accident involving a horse. Tremayne fell from his animal and broke his neck. Mr. Arthur Reese testified that he saw the subject fall."

"Reese saw the accident?" Jessie asked.

Continuing his by-rote account of the proceedings at the inquest, his eyes fixed on a point halfway between Ki and Jessie, Bowdeen continued. "Mr. Reese was riding with Mr. Tremayne when the accident occurred. They were both on their way home from the Empire Saloon when the accident occurred. There were no other witnesses since the hour was late and the streets were empty. Coroner's examination of the remains confirms that deceased died of a broken neck."

"There was no evidence of foul play?" Jessie asked.

"Foul play?" repeated Bowdeen as he put down the lamp that was wavering in his trembling hand. "Whatever do you mean by that? Of course there was no evidence of foul play."

"Are you sure somebody didn't strangle Tremayne?" Ki asked. "I mean somebody strong enough could have broken the man's neck."

"I repeat: there is no evidence of foul play. Mr. Reese would have reported same had there been any."

"Unless Mr. Reese was the foul player," Jessie said sweetly.

"How dare you?" Bowdeen cried. "Mr. Reese is an upstanding citizen of this town. A man of most excellent reputation."

"We'd heard that when Mr. Tremayne had his accident," Ki said, "he was deeply in debt to Mr. Reese. Is that true?"

"That is outside my official province," Bowdeen declared haughtily. "But," he added, "I have heard talk that would suggest such was indeed the case, yes. But surely you are not suggesting that Mr. Reese had anything to do with Mr. Tremayne's fall from his horse."

When neither Ki nor Jessie said anything, Bowdeen continued, "Tremayne was drunk at the time of the accident."

"You're sure of that?" Ki asked.

"Mr. Reese so testified at the inquest."

"Let me ask you something, Mr. Bowdeen." Ki stroked his chin. "Did Jack Radcliff testify at your coroner's inquest?"

"No."

"Why not?"

"He was not present when the accident occurred."

"But didn't you think that he could have confirmed Mr. Reese's testimony concerning Mr. Tremayne's alleged intoxication?"

"There was no reason to doubt Mr. Reese's testimony, therefore, no reason to call Mr. Radcliff to substantiate that testimony."

"You seem to have run a rather casual inquiry, Mr. Bowdeen," Jessie observed. "Was the same casual procedure followed during the inquest following the death of Brent Latrobe?"

"I resent the implication of your remark, Miss Starbuck," Bowdeen huffed. "The inquest following Mr. Latrobe's suicide was not casual, as you so offensively label Mr. Tremayne's. It followed standard procedures. Marshal Hayes testified at that proceeding to what he found that night. I also testified. It was clearly an open and shut case. Mr. Latrobe was found hanging from a rope that was tied to a doorknob and looped over the top of the door. He had stood on a stool that he subsequently kicked out from under him."

"Another man dead of a broken neck," Ki interjected.

Bowdeen refused to look at him.

"I wonder what we would discover about Brent Latrobe's death," Jessie mused, "if we were to obtain a court order to have the body exhumed."

"There is no earthly reason for such an action!" Bowdeen exclaimed shrilly. "The man hanged himself. What possible reason would you—or anyone else, for that matter—have to exhume Latrobe's body?"

"I'll give you a reason," Ki said. "To see if there were any bullet holes in Latrobe's body."

"As there are in the body of Charles Tremayne," Jessie quickly added. "We broke into your office tonight, Bowdeen and we saw Tremayne's corpse."

The coroner looked as if he were about to faint.

"Did you shoot Tremayne?" Ki asked, not believing for a minute that Bowdeen had done so but wanting to further unsettle the man in the hopes of getting him to tell the truth about what had happened to Tremayne.

"Me?" Bowdeen croaked. He began to shake his head. He began to wave his arms about aimlessly. "I didn't shoot him. I never shot anybody in my whole life. I don't carry a gun. I don't even know how to use one. Please, I—"

"Who did shoot him?" Jessie asked.

"I don't know."

"You do know," Ki snapped. He seized a fistful of Bowdeen's flannel nightshirt and pulled the coroner close to him. "Who did it, Bowdeen?"

"I didn't have anything to do with it."

"Who shot Tremayne?" Ki persisted, giving the coroner a shake that caused his teeth to click together.

"Don't hurt me," Bowdeen pleaded. "I'm not a well man. My heart—"

Ki shook him again.

"Are you going to kill him, Ki?" Jessie asked, affecting alarm.

Bowdeen let out an agonized moan. "It was . . . it was—"

Ki shook him a third time.

". . . Reese."

Ki let Bowdeen go. "We learned from Jack Radcliff, before Reese's sidekick, Roark, killed him, that Tremayne won big at poker the night he was shot to death—by Reese, you say. Reese claims he won everything from Tremayne and has an IOU to prove it. What about that, Bowdeen?"

"I only know what Reese told me afterward. He and Reese left the Empire Saloon together. They were both supposedly heading home. But Reese had other things in mind. He drew on Tremayne and forced him to ride out of town where he made Tremayne write out and sign an IOU pledging his real estate holdings to Reese to cover a fictitious gambling debt that didn't exist. Reese told Tremayne he wouldn't kill him if he did as he was told. But as soon as Tremayne signed the IOU Reese shot him to death. Then he came to me and told me to make sure the death was recorded as an accident—a fall from a horse."

"And you went along with Reese," Jessie said, disgust stiffening her tone. "Why?"

Bowdeen turned stricken eyes on her. "I had to. Reese said he would kill *me* if I didn't."

"Did you go along with Reese in the matter of Brent Latrobe's death too?" Jessie asked.

Bowdeen hesitated for a moment. He started to shake his head but instead said in a barely audible voice, "What's the use? In for a penny, in for a pound. Yes, I went along with Reese that time too for the same reason. Because I wanted to live. Reese said he'd kill me if I didn't cooperate."

"Then Mr. Latrobe didn't commit suicide?" Ki inquired.

"No, he didn't. Reese had Roark set up the suicide scene after Reese had shot Latrobe to death in his office."

"Did Reese really lend money to Latrobe before he died?" Jessie asked.

"No. Reese faked those drafts he claims prove he loaned money to Latrobe. He had them processed through Addison Chaney's bank—"

"Wait a minute," Ki said. "How could he do that?"

"Easily. Chaney was in on the deal with Reese. So was Lon Curlew. The three of them intended to own every head of cattle and every profitable piece of property from here to the Nations before they were through. Latrobe was the first man they killed for what he owned. Tremayne was the second."

"We saw a mortgage on the Latrobe homestead that had

169

been signed by Latrobe in Curlew's strong box," Jessie said. "Was that—"

"Before Reese killed Latrobe," Bowdeen said in a voice that suddenly sounded tired, "he made him sign his stock over to Curlew just as he had made Latrobe endorse the two drafts he had prepared and sign the mortgage turning his homestead over to Addison Chaney. Reese said he would kill him if he didn't sign. Latrobe signed. Then Reese shot him to death. Just as he did later with Tremayne."

Ki whistled through his teeth. "Slick."

"I can think of one or two other words to describe Reese's operation," Jessie commented bitterly. "Despicable, for one."

"Get dressed, Bowdeen," Ki ordered.

"Dressed? What for?"

"You're going with us."

"Where?"

"To the marshal. You committed crimes. You're going to pay for them."

Bowdeen didn't move.

Jessie slowly drew her derringer form a pocket of her deerskin jacket. "Mr. Bowdeen, I want to tell you something. Brent Latrobe was a very dear friend of mine. If you don't get dressed and come with us—right now—I am going to blow a hole in your head."

Bowdeen, escorted by Ki, quickly left the room and climbed the stairs to the second floor.

The coroner led Jessie and Ki to the home of Marshal Buck Hayes where Ki pounded on a door for the second time that night.

This time the door was opened almost at once by a fully-dressed and wide-awake Hayes.

His face was drawn as if he had spent a sleepless night.

There were dark patches under his eyes and his lips quivered like a man coming off a long drunk or one who was about to cry. When he had thrown open the door, there had been an expression of what might have been hope on his face. But when he saw who was standing on his porch that expression faded and his eyes went blank.

"We want this man locked up, Marshal," Jessie announced, indicating the coroner.

"He's an accomplice to murder," Ki explained.

Hayes peered past the trio on his doorstep as if he were searching for something—or someone—in the night.

"Did you hear us, Marshal?" Jessie asked. "Bowdeen here tried to cover up the murders of Brent Latrobe and Charles Tremayne."

Hayes stared wordlessly at Bowdeen who matched the marshal's silence. "What's this all about?" he asked finally.

Jessie told him what she and Ki had discovered when they broke into Bowdeen's office earlier in the night.

When she had finished, Hayes's shoulders seemed to droop. He seemed to shrink. He looked at Bowdeen and then turned and walked unsteadily into the dark house.

Jessie and Ki, prodding the coroner into the house in front of them followed Hayes into the house.

Bowdeen cursed as he collided with a piece of furniture he had been unable to see because of the fact that no lamps burned inside the house.

"Light a lamp, Buck, so we can see where we are," Bowdeen said, his voice seemingly disembodied in the darkness.

Hayes obediently struck a match and lit a lamp. He stood there with the match burning in his hand, staring at the lamp he had lit as if he had never seen it before. When the match burned his fingers, he dropped it.

Ki stepped forward and stamped it out before it could set fire to the pegged planking that formed the floor.

171

"Marshal, what's wrong with you?" Ki asked, sure that something was definitely wrong with the man who looked like a ghost and moved like a broken machine.

Before Hayes could respond, Bowdeen said, "Tell them, Buck. They'll find out anyway sooner or later."

"Tell us what?" Jessie asked Hayes.

The marshal reached out and gripped the edge of a table as if to steady himself. "I was in on it," he said at last. "The same as Bowdeen was."

"You were also an accomplice to the murders of Latrobe and Tremayne?" Jessie asked, not sure of what Hayes had meant by his remarks.

"That's right."

"Why'd you go along with Reese?" an incredulous Ki asked. "Were you afraid he'd kill you if you didn't? Bowdeen says that's the reason he covered up the killings for Reese."

"No, I wasn't afraid Reese would kill me. In fact, there were times I wish he had killed me." Hayes looked directly at Ki. "Twenty years ago, before Opal was born, I killed a man. It happened in Arizona Territory. It was self-defense, I swear it was, but I was tried and convicted of murder in the first degree. They were going to hang me. But I escaped from jail.

"Somehow or other Reese found out about the warrant outstanding for my arrest a month ago. He's been using it to force me to go along with his schemes, to cover up for him, to lie—"

"As you lied about finding Brent Latrobe hanged in his office," an angry Jessie interrupted.

"That's right. Reese had shot him after forcing him to sign those two drafts. Then he sent Reese for me and Bowdeen and together we rigged the fake suicide."

"You spoke of covering up for Reese a moment ago," Ki said. "You also covered up for Roark when he killed

Jack Radcliff, didn't you? You knew it was cold-blooded murder but you went ahead and defended Roark's action."

"I had to. Reese wanted Radcliff killed. I knew that and I knew he had sent Roark out to get him."

Hayes swallowed hard. "But that's not the worst thing I did to keep Reese from having me arrested and sent back to prison to hang. God knows, I had sunk pretty low but tonight—tonight was the worst yet."

"What happened?" Ki prompted.

For a moment, Hayes couldn't speak. Then, getting hold of himself, he said, "Reese sent Roark here tonight. He wanted—Reese did—my daughter. He'd been making advances to Opal for some time now—almost since the day he first saw her after she got back here from the East. But she wouldn't give him the time of day.

"When Roark came here tonight and told Opal that Reese wanted to see her, she told him that she wasn't the least bit interested in seeing Reese. Roark told her that she had better make herself interested or she'd be sorry. Opal asked him what he meant by that remark. Roark just grinned and told her to ask me.

"I couldn't tell her about the killing—about me having been in prison, about the fact that I was a wanted man and would hang if I was ever caught again.

"I told her—" Hayes sobbed, "—to go with Roark. I'll never forget the look on her face when I told her that. She looked at me as if I had just struck her. But she didn't say anything, not a word. She just went with Roark."

Silence followed Hayes's account of what had happened in the house earlier.

Ki broke it with, "I'm going after Opal. And Reese."

"Wait a minute, Ki." Jessie said. "Marshal, Tess Latrobe has arranged with Governor Kirkland for a special prosecutor to investigate the cause of her husband's death. My guess is that if you and Bowdeen will testify against

Reese, Chaney and Curlew, you both might be able to strike a deal with the prosecutor concerning your own roles in this affair. Would you be willing to do that?"

"I would," Bowdeen said without hesitation.

"If I did that," Hayes said, "I'd have to admit that I'm a wanted man and that there's a rope waiting for me in Arizona Territory."

"Tess Latrobe is a good friend of Governor Kirkland," Jessie said. "I think she could use her influence with him to strike a deal with the Arizona authorities to get your death sentence commuted. Of course, I can't make either one of you any promises. But if I were you I'd be happy to testify for the prosecution."

"I'll do it," Hayes said. "I want to see that bastard, Reese—I beg your pardon, Miss Starbuck—hang for what he's done."

"Do you want to come with me and help get Opal away from Reese, Marshal?" Ki asked and received an approving glance from Jessie.

Hayes seemed to suddenly grow in stature. "You bet your boots I do!"

"Mr. Bowdeen," Jessie said, "I suggest that you go the the Latrobe ranch and wait for us there. At the ranch you'll be out of harm's way. We wouldn't want anything to happen to one of the star witnesses against Reese and the others."

When a grateful Bowdeen had gone, Hayes said, "There's one thing I didn't mention before."

"What was that?" Jessie asked.

"Roark, just before he left here with Opal, told me that Reese wasn't the only one interested in my daughter. So were Addison Chaney and Lon Curlew he said, and since they were all meeting tonight at Reese's house to plan their next move, maybe they'd get a crack at Opal too. That's how he put it—'maybe they'd get a crack at Opal too.' So if they're still at Reese's place when we get there, we'll have more than just Reese to contend with."

"That's fine with me," Ki said as he put his hand in the pocket of his leather vest and felt the reassuring presence there of his *shuriken*, his five-bladed throwing stars. "Maybe we can kill three birds with one stone."

"Four if Roark is also there," Jessie said.

Chapter 12

When Jessie, Ki, and Hayes arrived at Reese's house, which was a three-story clapboard building with a wide veranda, they found that there were lights on both downstairs and in one of the upstairs rooms.

"Let's take a look inside," Ki suggested.

They went around to the right side of the house and stopped in front of an open window.

Inside the large parlor they saw Reese, Curlew, and Chaney. All three were seated around a table in the middle of the room. A whiskey bottle and three empty glasses sat on the table as did an oblong ashtray which was filled with cigar butts. All the men were in their shirt sleeves. Curlew was showing a document to Chaney who tapped a pencil against his teeth as he perused it.

"You're right, Curlew," Chaney said, touching the point of his pencil to the paper the stockman was displaying. "Jessup is a pigeon ripe for the plucking."

"Then we agree," said Reese, "that we should go after Art Jessup's freighting company next."

"He's by far the biggest teamster in the state of Texas,"

Curlew stated. "Once we have control of his outfit, we can charge any freighting fees we like."

"Not so fast," said Chaney. "There's Barstow's Red Arrow Line. It's no small potatoes, and it runs some of the same routes Jessup's line does. That could be a problem."

"It won't be a problem," Reese said with assurance. "I'll see to it that Roark and some of his boys puts Barstow out of business once we've got control of the Jessup operation. Then we can charge whatever fees we like because we'll have a monopoly on the state's freighting business which will force shippers to pay whatever we choose to charge."

"What's it going to be this time?" Chaney asked Reese.

"You mean what will be the manner of Jessup's demise? He could be run over and killed by a carriage. How does that sound?"

"It will have to be done at night when there's no one around," Curlew said. "And of course it will be a case of the carriage driver having failed to stop so that the culprit will never be found. Who's going to drive the carriage?"

"Roark will," Reese replied. Turning to Curlew, he said, "How soon can you have all the necessary papers drawn up?"

"By noon tomorrow," Curlew answered. "Now, let me be sure I've got everything straight. You want a draft of mine for thirty thousand dollars made out to Jessup. Also a draft from your office drawn on Chaney's bank in the amount of another forty thousand dollars. And a lien on Jessup's freight business issued by me in exchange for a payment of twenty-five thousand in cash."

"That's about it," Reese said. He was about to remove the tip from a cigar when he said, "I don't need another nail in my coffin." He rose and stretched. "I think it's high time we treated ourselves to a little entertainment, gentlemen. The lady's been waiting on us long enough, I think.

We really shouldn't keep her waiting any longer. If there are no objections, I'll go first."

There were no objections.

"You two can decide between yourselves who'll be second and third on line," Reese said. As if to punctuate his remark, he snapped his braces and then headed for the hall beyond the parlor.

Outside the window, Ki grabbed Hayes by the shoulder and hissed, "Where's Jessie?"

"I don't know. She was here a minute ago."

"Here I am," Jessie said, materializing out of the darkness. "I went to check the back door. It's unlocked. While you two are going in the front, I'll go in the back. We'll outflank them once we get inside."

"There's a minor complication," Ki said. "Reese has gone upstairs—"

"Let's move, Ki!" an obviously upset Hayes said. "You know why Reese has gone upstairs. You heard what he said."

"Opal?" Jessie asked.

Ki nodded. "Let's go. We'll count to forty. That will give us all time to get into position. Then we move."

Jessie disappeared in the darkness.

Ki and Hayes went around the veranda and up the front steps to the front door. Hayes knocked on the door.

"Hello, in there!" he yelled, fidgeting from one foot to the other as he continued his pounding. "Open the door!"

It was Chaney who opened it. "Hayes! What the hell are you doing here?"

"I've come to take my daughter home. Get out of my way, Chaney."

Hayes pushed his way past the startled banker who became even more startled when he saw Ki move in right behind the marshal and then Jessie enter the room from the rear of the house, her derringer in her hand.

"Don't make a sound," Ki warned both Chaney and Curlew. "If you do, you're in trouble."

"Just what the hell do you think you're trying to pull, Hayes?" Chaney barked. "If you try to take Opal away from us, Reese will blow the whistle on you for sure, and you'll swing in the Arizona sun for the felon that you are."

"I may be a felon," Hayes muttered through clenched teeth, "but I'm no swine which is what you three are."

Curlew yelled, *"Reese!"*

The name was no sooner out of his mouth than Jessie brought her derringer down on the man's head.

As Curlew fell unconscious to the floor, there was the sound of a scuffle on the second floor.

"Keep your eye on these two," Ki told Jessie before sprinting out of the room past an inlaid writing desk that had an ivory-handled paper opener on its surface. Hayes was right behind him.

When they reached the landing on the second floor, the sound of a woman's scream guided them to a bedroom at the end of a short hall.

Ki was the first to enter the bedroom, but Hayes was not far behind him.

Reese was kneeling on the bed and straddling Opal who lay on her back beneath him. Her body twisted back and forth beneath her captor, but he had a firm grip on her wrists so she could not escape him.

Ki reached the bed in two swift strides. He seized Reese by the shoulders and jerked the man violently backward. As Reese was ripped free of Opal, Hayes reached the bed and wrapped his arms around his daughter whose blue blouse had been torn and whose long blue skirt had been pulled down around her thighs.

Ki spun Reese around. Before the man could utter a word, Ki slammed him up against the wall. Holding a fistful of the man's linen shirt, Ki held him there, wanting to kill him, but wanting to make the man suffer first.

"Let me go!" Reese bellowed, grappling with Ki who held his ground and his prisoner in place. "I'll kill you, you—"

Ki suddenly let go of Reese who stared at him in surprise for a moment. Then Reese, lunged for Ki. Ki turned adroitly to the left. He raised his right leg, then shot it forward so that his stiff foot struck Reese in the throat.

Reese staggered backward, holding his throat in both hands, his tongue protruding from his mouth, his face turning blue.

Ki, conscious of Opal's frantic weeping coming from behind him, ordered Hayes to get his daughter out of the room. When Hayes, holding Opal close to him, had left the room, Ki gave the gagging Reese a shove that sent him careening out of the room into the hall.

"Downstairs," Ki ordered, following in Reese's footsteps. Hayes and Opal were, he noted, already halfway down the staircase.

Reese obediently began his descent with Ki right behind him. But halfway down, Reese suddenly turned and threw a right jab at Ki. The blow caught Ki in the gut and knocked the wind out of him. Reese tried to follow up with a left hook but Ki shunted the blow aside with a wide sweep of his right arm. Then he brought his knee up fast, catching Reese under the chin with his kneecap. Reese's head snapped backward and then his entire body was leaning backward at a precarious forty-five degree angle. An instant later, windmilling his arms helplessly, he toppled down the staircase to lie on the ground floor landing in a crumpled and totally senseless heap. On the way down, he had struck his head on a wooden footstool that sat in front of a ladder-back chair in the hall.

Ki completed his descent. At the landing, he stepped over Reese's body and went into the parlor.

"You killed him!" Curlew, who had regained consciousness, cried. He stared in horror at Reese who had not
stirred since his fall.

"Foreign savage!" exclaimed an indignant Chaney.

Ki ignored them both. He went over to where Hayes
was standing with Opal in his arms, her face hidden, as she
continued to sob softly.

When he placed a gentle hand on her shoulder, he was
saddened by the fact that she flinched from him in fear.

"Opal, it's me! Ki."

Her sobbing gradually ceased. She lifted her head and
turned so that she could see him. "Oh, Ki!" she cried, a
stricken expression on her tear-stained face.

"You're all right," he whispered to her. "You'll be fine.
It's over now, all of it."

"No, it's not!" a male voice roared from across the
room.

Ki spun around to see Roark, gun in hand, standing at
the rear entrance to the room. He remained motionless as
Roark strode forward before Jessie could turn and grabbed
her around the neck from behind, causing her to drop her
gun.

"Where the hell have you been?" Chaney shouted at
Roark. "You were supposed to be back here an hour ago.
My God, man, how long does it take to bring a growler of
beer back from the Empire Saloon?"

"Take it slow and easy, gents," Roark barked. "I got the
growler you sent me for so don't wet your pants worrying
about that. It's out back.

"Now, to answer your question, Chaney. I stopped on
the way back from the Empire to dally with a little lady
who's as much of a foreigner in this country as that Jap
over there is. Only this lady's from Mexico. Hot as a ta-
male, is my Rosa Cortez." Roark laughed and then asked,
"What are these people doing here, Chaney?"

"They came for Opal Hayes."

"That's not all we came for," Ki said cooly. "We also came to take the lot of you into custody for murder. Specifically, for the murders of Brent Latrobe and Charles Tremayne and, in your case, Roark, for the murder of Jack Radcliff."

Jessie clawed at Roark's arm as the man broke into a loud fit of laughter, but she failed to free herself.

"*You* are going to take *us* into custody?" Roark said when his laughter had subsided. "Now that is truly the joke of the century!"

A pale and drawn Lon Curlew was staring at Ki. Then he switched his attention to Roark. "Shoot them!" he cried shrilly, his finger pointing first at Ki, then at Hayes and Opal, then at Jessie. "Kill them all!" he shrieked. "They'll see us all hang if we let them live!"

"Go ahead and shoot, Curlew," Roark said. "Use that gun the lady dropped."

For a moment, Curlew didn't move. Then, his cane striking the floor in an uneven rhythm, he crossed to where Jessie's derringer lay on the floor. He bent down and picked it up.

He turned and, without hesitation, fired at Ki.

But Ki, anticipating just such an action on Curlew's part, had dropped to a crouching position an instant before Curlew fired and so was unhurt.

Curlew, red-faced now with frustration, took aim and fired the one remaining bullet in Jessie's gun. It too missed Ki who, because Curlew had been aiming low to hit him where he crouched, had leaped high into the air and the bullet bit into the wall directly behind where he had been only a moment before.

"Roark, you kill him!" Curlew screamed, pointing a shaking finger at Ki.

Ki tensed, his wary eyes on Roark.

Roark raised his gun, still holding Jessie in a choke hold.

Jessie suddenly raised her right foot and brought the heel of her boot down hard on Roark's instep.

The man howled in pain and released his hold on her.

She dashed across the room toward Curlew. She shoved him backward and, as he fell over a stuffed chair, she seized his cane. She turned and, using the cane as a make-shift version of the *jo*—the short staff used often as a weapon in the martial arts—sprang toward Roark.

The man saw her coming, but because of the speed with which she moved Roark was unable to get off a single shot before the cane in Jessie's hand struck him on the side of the head.

Roark was obviously dazed by the blow, but he retained consciousness.

Jessie was about to strike him again when Ki shouted, "Look out!"

Before Ki could move, a recovered Reese, whom Ki had just caught sight of out of the corner of his eye, threw a wooden footstool across the room.

It hit Jessie hard and knocked the *jo* from her hand. She fell back against the wall.

Roark smirked and took aim at her.

Ki swiftly removed one of his *shuriken* from the pocket of his vest. He threw it in a graceful but deadly arc and watched impassively as it struck the left side of Roark's head and three of its five blades dug deep into his brain.

Roark's gun went off harmlessly, hitting no one. He jerked spasmodically and then let go of his revolver. It fell to the floor. A moment later, so did he. He lay there motionless, his life lost to him, lamplight glinting on the blades of Ki's *shuriken* that protruded so grotesquely from his skull.

A shot roared in the room.

Ki turned, saw Hayes's smoking gun, turned the other way, saw Reese, the paper opener he had taken from his writing desk clutched in his hand, crumple and fall to his knees while holding his shoulder from which blood was flowing and staining his shirt.

"He was all set to go for you," Hayes said quietly. "I had to stop him."

"I'm grateful to you, Marshal," Ki said sincerely. He went to Jessie and asked, "Are you badly hurt?"

"It would take more than a footstool to hurt me badly," Jessie replied. "But I do smart some, I'll admit."

"I'll lock these men up in the jail," Hayes said. "I'll send somebody for Doc Swinton so he can have a look at Reese though, to tell the plain truth, I'd as soon let him bleed to death as do that."

The marshal, gun in hand and his arm around Opal, started to march Curlew, Chaney and a quietly cursing Reese out of the house. Before he reached the front door, Opal left his side and went to where Ki and Jessie were standing.

Without any hesitation, she threw her arms around Ki and kissed him. "Thank you for what you did for me," she whispered. "I love you for it, Ki. And for other reasons as well. But him"—she turned to face her father who was waiting for her in the hall—"him I hate. I'll never forgive him for ordering me to go with Roark tonight. Never!"

"Marshal," Ki called out. "There's something I think you'd better clear up here and clear it up fast. Tell your daughter why you sent her to Reese tonight. Tell her everything."

"I will," Hayes promised.

"Hear him out, Opal," Ki said. "Then you'll understand, and you won't hate your father. He's just a man which, I've learned, means he's both good and bad. He has his fears and he has his sorrows. I can tell you one thing

184

about him for sure. He loves you with all his heart."

Opal stared long and hard at Ki. She was about to say something but instead turned and left with her father.

Jessie said, "I think it's time we went back to the ranch and had a talk with Tess, don't you, Ki?"

"I do."

As they started for the door, leaving Roark's corpse lying on the floor behind them, Ki said, "I want to thank you for keeping Roark from putting a hole or two in my hide."

"You're welcome. I'm always glad to do a favor for a friend."

The following afternoon, Jessie and Ki stood on the platform of the Texas and Pacific's depot with Tess between them as they waited for the westbound train.

"Do you think those three men will hang for what they did?" Tess asked.

"Reese probably will," Jessie speculated. "Chaney and Curlew will probably do time—a lot of it."

"I'm so glad it's over," Tess said. "And I'm so glad you two came when I needed your help and put an end to what was going on. Oh, that reminds me." Tess rooted in her reticule and came up with a folded piece of paper which she handed to Jessie. "One of Art Jessup's men brought this over early this morning. He said that Art said it was for—now how did he put it? Oh, yes, I remember. He said it was for 'the lady who saved my life and livelihood.'"

"Art Jessup?" Jessie took the paper from Tess.

"We overheard Reese and the others plotting to kill him and take over his freighting business," Ki reminded Jessie.

"Oh, of course. The name didn't register at first." She unfolded the paper and read the handwritten message Jessup had sent her.

"Mr. Jessup says I'm to show this paper to his agents

whenever Starbuck Enterprises wants to ship freight within Texas and there will be no charge for the service. Now, isn't that nice of him?"

"Not all of our El Paso businessmen are merchants of death like Reese and his cohorts were," Tess said.

"That's an apt way of putting it," Ki remarked. "That's exactly what those three scoundrels really were—death merchants."

"Listen," Tess said. "Isn't that the train whistle I hear in the distance?"

"It is," Jessie said.

"I do hope you'll be able to get some sleep on the trip home," Tess, told Jessie. "I saw you and Cass Henderson ride out early this morning so I know you didn't get much sleep during the night."

"Yes. Well, Cass was up when we got back last night and he suggested to me then that we go for an early morning ride."

Ki, as Jessie glanced at him, simply nodded soberly. But his eyes twinkled.

"Ki!"

He turned at the sound of his name being called and saw Opal hurrying along the platform toward him.

When she reached him, she blurted out, "I was picking up a package at the depot for papa just now when I saw you. I planned to come to the ranch later to tell you that papa explained everything to me. He said he talked this morning with Mr. Richard Defoe, the special prosecutor looking into the deaths of Mr. Latrobe and Mr. Tremayne. Mr. Defoe said our governor, Mr. Kirkland, had telegraphed the governor of Arizona Territory, and he has agreed to grant papa a pardon for the crime he was convicted of there twenty years ago. Especially since papa saved your life and will be, as will be Mr. Bowdeen, testifying against Reese and his fellow defendants."

"That's the best news I've heard in a whole month of Sundays," Ki said.

He couldn't understand the next words Opal spoke because the train that came grinding and whistling into the depot drowned them out. But he did understand her feelings when she threw her arms around him and hugged him until he was breathless.

"Ki, come on!" Jessie cried from the train she had boarded.

Opal released him and he climbed aboard. Minutes later, as the train pulled out of the depot, he and Jessie waved a farewell through the window to Tess and Opal.

Watch for

LONE STAR AND THE COMSTOCK CROSS FIRE

seventy-eighth novel in the exciting
LONE STAR
series from Jove

coming in February!